PRAISE FOR
KRIPPENDORF'S TRIBE

"WILD AND RAUNCHY . . . [Parkin's] cockeyed view of some especially daft corners of our life and times is original, exceptionally well-realized—and funny."—*People*

"A HILARIOUS BOOK you dare not read if sidesplitting laughter isn't your cup of tea. . . . Families and academics may never be the same."—*Newsday*

"[*Krippendorf's Tribe*] had me laughing on the very first page and quite regularly thereafter."—*The Plain Dealer* (Cleveland)

"PARKIN KEEPS US IN PERPETUAL STITCHES."—*Chicago Tribune*

"A SURPRISING KIND OF MADCAP *MARY POPPINS*."—*The New York Times Book Review*

"Nastier than Amis' *Lucky Jim*, fiercer than Bradbury's *The History of Man*. . . . Anthropology may never recover."—*Newsweek*

BOOKS BY FRANK PARKIN

Krippendorf's Tribe

Frank Parkin

Delta
Trade Paperbacks

A Delta Book
Published by
Dell Publishing
a division of
Bantam Doubleday Dell Publishing Group, Inc.
1540 Broadway
New York, New York 10036

ISBN: 0-385-33281-5

Reprinted by arrangement with Atheneum

Manufactured in the United States of America
Published simultaneously in Canada

March 1998

10 9 8 7 6 5 4 3 2 1

BVG

To Kathy

One

Krippendorf sat on the edge of his daughter's bed, sniffing through a pile of her multicoloured knickers. He felt reasonably sure that his sole motive for doing this was to sort out the ones that needed washing. He let them flutter one by one into an Ali Baba laundry basket that was already half-filled with his sons' glutinous socks and Tottenham Hotspur tee-shirts. He had earlier noted the operation of the iron law that decreed that no two children's socks in any pile ever made a pair. All the odd socks were preserved in a dark cupboard beneath the stairs as though to provide future archaeologists with firm evidence for the evolution of a small one-legged race.

For a moment or two he contemplated probing through the heap of rubble beneath the bed in search of other things to wash. He raked it tentatively with his bare toes before extracting something that might have been one of his daughter's attempts at a tie-and-dye skirt or a rag for wiping brushes on. He weighed up the probabilities, smelled it, and added it to the pile. The room was hot and stuffy and he fiddled with the catch on the window, forgetting it was permanently stuck. Soon he would repair it, after he had fixed the leaking bidet and the wobbly leg on the piano stool. He stood by the window gazing down at the reproachful neatness of his neighbours' gardens, scratching himself mechanically through his silk pyjamas. Presently, the church clock struck an unintelligible hour. He wrapped both arms around the laundry basket like a

7

foreign sailor dancing with a barmaid and picked his way downstairs.

He began sorting out the washing into separate piles, following the multilingual instructions on the labels. After a while he gave this up, stuffed everything into the machine and switched it to the only programme that he ever used. He worked with unnecessary concentration, whistling fiercely on a single high-pitched note, as though to drown out the noise of the children fighting in the kitchen. A heavy thud immediately above his head was followed by a shriek of laughter or pain that was in turn succeeded by a series of unevenly spaced but interconnected sobs. The sobs became louder and more coherently orchestrated as Edmund approached. His seven-year-old son had a worryingly pale triangular face from which long skeins of snot were now hanging.

'Shelley thumped me,' he blubbered, wiping his nose on his Snoopy vest. 'She hit me with the electric wok.'

'That really is too bad of her,' Krippendorf complained. 'She knows very well the guarantee has expired.' He picked up his son and cradled him in his arms. There was a patch of red on his forehead and the first signs of swelling. Krippendorf dabbed gently at it with a damp handkerchief and carefully removed the surrounding gobbets of Marmite and chunky peanut butter. Edmund's sobs gradually subsided and he allowed himself to be carried back to the kitchen.

Shelley was scraping burnt toast over the sink with the back of the breadknife. 'He asked for it,' she said, without turning. 'He stole the batteries from my vibrator.' She gave a toss of her head that was not quite in keeping with the shortness of her hair. This was dyed magenta at the front and dark green at the back and seemed to have been mangled in industrial machinery. She sat at the table and nibbled with exaggerated delicacy at her butterless toast.

'Shelley,' Krippendorf enquired, 'what exactly are you wearing?'

8

His daughter looked at him as though he had suddenly, but not unexpectedly, become deranged. 'It's a dress. I'm wearing a dress.'

He peered more closely. 'It looks very much like baking foil.'

'That's right,' she said, enunciating her words with precision, 'it is baking foil. It is a dress made of baking foil.' She pointed to her cup and to her plate. 'And this is a cup, and this is a plate.'

'Shelley, I needed that foil for the roast chicken.'

For a moment she looked thoughtful, but not contrite. 'When are we having roast chicken?'

'Sunday luncheon.'

'That's all right, you can have it back by then.'

Still clutching Edmund, he collected the morning mail and the newspaper off the mat and made himself a cup of instant coffee. The headlines were only marginally different from yesterday's headlines. Peace talks in the Middle East were still poised at the same critical stage; the hostages were still being held on the runway; the Black Death was still ravaging Milton Keynes; the weather forecast was still scattered showers followed by more persistent rain from the north. He remembered the washing was still hanging on the line. It had now been hanging out for five days and nights, alternating between wetness and dampness. Surreptitiously he disengaged himself from Edmund, put on his carpet slippers and Samurai dresing-gown, and shuffled into the garden.

Almost at once his neighbour's head appeared above the fence next to the failed marrow bed. 'Could I have a word, Mr K.?' she said. 'It's about your boy, Mickey.' Only her face was visible above the fairly low fence.

'Not now, Mrs O'Shea. I have to get the children off to school.' He went quickly along the line unpegging damp clothes.

'He's been setting light to my cat again.' A knobbly hand appeared on either side of her face and gripped the fence as though she was about to haul herself over. 'He's been using napalm.'

'Napalm?' Krippendorf unpegged the last pair of hipster jeans and hurried to the back door.

'He makes it from paraffin and golden syrup and shoots it out of his bicycle pump.'

He shut the back door behind him with his foot and went in search of Mickey. At the foot of the stairs he found Edmund, wearing nothing but a vest, his face buried in a comic. 'Edmund, for goodness sake, it has passed eight-thirty. Will you please get dressed.'

Without looking up from his comic, Edmund said, 'I need clean underpants.'

'I have just put a clean pair in your room.'

'They're the wrong ones.'

'What?'

'I need my Snoopy ones.'

'They are still damp. Your Incredible Hulk ones will have to suffice.'

For the first time Edmund raised his eyes from the comic. 'I've got my Snoopy vest on, right?'

'I cannot deny it.'

'Well then. I can't wear Incredible Hulk underpants with a Snoopy vest. Don't be so ridiculous.'

Krippendorf stared down at his large feet. Encased in furry brown carpet slippers they looked even larger and somehow meaningless. For a moment he toyed with the idea of taking a principled stand on the underpants question, but then gradually became reconciled to the prospect of one more defeat for the cause of rationality. He extracted the Snoopy underpants from the pile of damp laundry and put them in the oven on gas mark four.

Shelley was still sitting at the kitchen table, painting her fingernails different colours. 'Where is Mickey?' he asked. She shrugged, moving her shoulders the barest minimum for the gesture to qualify as a shrug.

'You ought to be off,' he said. 'Look at the time.'

She was blowing on the ends of her fingers and shaking them dry. There was a smell of something vaguely explosive.

'Shelley, do you hear me? Will you please get your shoes on. You will be late for school again and I cannot fabricate another note.'

Shelley propped a bare foot against the edge of the table and began painting her toenails. 'Wake up, Jim-Jam,' she said wearily. 'It's Saturday.'

From somewhere in the far distance he could hear the peal of bells. The sound moved closer and closer while he remained quite still. He was in a yacht, or it might have been a gondola, suspended motionless on the water. The darkness pressed against his face like a cold hand. He opened his eyes, shielding them with a raised arm. The telephone was ringing and he waited for it to stop. He knew it would not stop. He climbed out of bed and crept downstairs, holding on to the banister all the way.

'Hello?' He mumbled his number.

'Pardon me?' said a voice at the other end.

He repeated the number, including the London prefix.

'Is that the Yardley household?'

'It is not.'

'Who am I speaking with please?' said the voice in what he now recognized to be an American accent.

'Krippendorf here. James Krippendorf.'

There was no response other than a sound like a starving man eating a stick of celery in the bath. He shook the receiver as if to clear the obstruction.

Presently someone said, 'Hello, I'd like to speak with Veronica Yardley.' It was a different voice this time, more authoritative but equally American.

'I am afraid you cannot. She is away.'

'Is that Mr Yardley?'

'No.' There was a momentary silence while this information was assimilated.

'Can you tell me where I can reach her? It's the *Los Angeles Times* here. It's urgent.'

'She is in Taiwan filming the factory riots.' Or was it Namibia, filming the guerilla bases?

'I see. Could you kindly ask her to ring this number as soon as she gets back.' The authoritative voice read out a long string of digits which Krippendorf did his best to copy down on the one small corner of the message board not already covered by Mickey's drawings of fat ladies being chased by matchstick men with erections.

'Thank you,' the voice said. 'And have a nice day.'

Krippendorf squinted at the clock. It was almost two-thirty.

He padded to the bathroom and struggled for a while with the safety top on his bottle of sleeping pills. When he saw his reflection in the splashback mirror he felt only mildly surprised at the puffiness of his eyes and the lines across his forehead. His hair was retreating in several quite different places on top while being pointlessly luxuriant at the back and sides. He bared his teeth at the mirror to assess the impact of the new trial-offer toothpaste that the children had made him buy on account of its allegedly toffeemint flavour. Then he pulled in his stomach and stepped on the bathroom scales. His weight was about right for a tall man, he thought, making due allowance for his silk pyjamas and Samurai dressing-gown. There was clearly no need yet to cut down on cigarettes or spread polyunsaturated fats upon his bread, or buy a navy-blue track-suit with a double white stripe along the sleeve.

Two hours later he was still wide awake. A dull grey light was leaking through the gap in the bedroom curtains and soon he could feel as well as hear the distant rumble of the Underground. He threw aside the covers and went up to the large converted attic that had recently become his study. It was too early for the central heating and he stood in the middle of the room flapping his arms against his sides as though in parody of a man trying to get warm. Puffing a small cigar, he unlocked the drawer of his desk and returned the key to its hiding place behind a framed photograph of the children looking miserable on a beach. He took from the drawer a manila folder containing a heavily emended manuscript which he proceeded to read with full concentration. His pen moved over the words as though he was counting them for a telegram. Some of his observations were really quite penetrating, he decided. The more he read the more impressed he became with his own mastery of the subject and the originality of his contribution to it. He took a clean sheet of paper, charged his pen with the brown ink he currently favoured, and began at once on the second draft.

THE SHELMIKEDMU OF THE AMAZON BASIN:
Moral Foundations of Political Economy

A unique feature of the social and economic organization of the Shelmikedmu, and one that is of particular interest to anthropological science, is the sexual division of labour. Among these people, the women are the chief breadwinners while the men are responsible for all domestic and household chores. From the onset of puberty girls are taught the arts of tracking, hunting and fishing by their mothers, while boys are given instruction by their fathers in the arcane skills of cooking, cleaning and washing. In all other Amazonian tribes young men seek to demonstrate their manhood by displays of prowess and bravery with spear and bow. Among the Shelmikedmu, however, they vie with one another to cook the tastiest manioc pudding or to get the brightest sparkle on their pots and pans.

Married men take immense pride in keeping the domestic hut spick and span. They are forever sweeping, scrubbing and polishing in the endeavour to impress their village neighbours. One of the most cutting insults one man can throw at another is to call him *ulqunxri-na tiqohxmopln* – literally, 'he of the greasy pots'. Fights frequently break out because of adverse comments made about the imperfect condition of a man's floor or his less than immaculate laundering of the family loincloths.

Domestic labour is one of the principal sources of self-esteem among the Shelmikedmu and, for this reason perhaps, is an exclusive male preserve. Hunting, and all the cognate activities surrounding it, is looked upon with scorn as *xnlxipu* – 'women's work'. It is held to be spiritually and morally unrewarding to engage in any kind of productive labour. Such work is thought to be deeply alienating, having none of the potential for self-realization and human creativity afforded by the cleaning, washing and cooking process. In Shelmikedmu eyes, the only fully rounded personality, the only truly complete human being, is one who sweeps in the morning, scrubs in the afternoon and cooks in the evening.

Krippendorf laid aside his pen and lit another small cigar. It was a popular brand advertised on television and, to his own distaste, he often found himself humming the catchy tune that accompanied the commercial. He paced about the room rubbing warmth into his hands, flexing his knees and gyrating his shoulders, before once again taking up his pen.

Shelmikedmu are perfectly well aware that neighbouring tribes arrange the division of labour along different lines from their own. But they are contemptuously dismissive of what they regard as effeminate social systems. Few things are able to provoke their derision more than the sight, or even the very thought, of a man holding a spear. Despite all this, there are certain indications that in an earlier phase of their development the Shelmikedmu divided male and female tasks along more conventional lines, though no man would dare to admit as much.

One such indication of this is provided by the annual Ceremony of the Brooms. This is the one and only occasion in the year on which women are permitted to handle cleaning and cooking utensils, and then in a purely ritual capacity. At daybreak on the morning of the ceremony each married woman appears at the entrance to the family compound. While her husband feigns sleep she seizes a prized domestic object – usually a long broom made of bamboo and palm fronds or, occasionally, a smaller hand broom. She then goes through the motions of sweeping the hut. At a certain point the village headman raises the alarm by banging on his cooking pots. Then men immediately rise from their beds, and a purely stylized tussle ensues for possession of the broom. The men are always victorious in this combat, and the women are ignominiously expelled from their huts, after which they once again take up their spears and bows.

Later, the men assemble for a triumphant parade around the village, holding their brooms aloft. They then proceed to the ancestral shrine for a thanksgiving ceremony and feast. This re-enactment of the expulsion of women from domestic labour concludes with a ritual purification of the brooms, presided over by the village elders.

The older women appear to accept their exclusion from housework with complete resignation, as though it were part of the natural order of things. Among the younger women, however, there are occasional mur-murings of discontent. Some of them have begun to ask why they should be denied access to the spiritually en-hancing activities of domestic labour and made instead to shoulder the burden of the breadwinner's role. The older women are shocked and disturbed by these heretical ideas and seek to persuade the younger women that there is nothing inherently degrading in productive work. The young women, for their part, accuse the older women of being blind to their own real interests and of being too much under the sway of the men's own beliefs that a woman's place is outside the home.

In some Shelmikedmu villages feelings have reached such a pitch that young women have openly rebelled against their condition. They have publicly burned their hunting gear and demanded the same cooking and cleaning opportunities as men. I witnessed several episodes of this kind throughout my stay, all of which provoked a violent reaction by the men as they sought to defend their domestic privileges.

Krippendorf pondered for a while over this last para-graph. He read it through several times and then, with some misgivings, crossed it out and wrote:

Despite the resentment undoubtedly felt by young Shelmikedmu women at their menial status, they have never shown any inclination to challenge openly the male domestic monopoly. Now and then a young woman may be seen swishing her bow to and fro in pathetic imitation of a sweeping motion; and once I observed a woman vigorously polishing a large stone with a tuft of grass. But apart from these symbolic, and probably unconscious, expressions of frustration women give every outward appearance of being recon-ciled to their lot.

'Yes please,' Veronica said, rattling the ice cubes in her otherwise empty whisky glass. She was reclining in the bath, a glass in one hand, a cigarette in the other, twiddling the taps with her feet. Krippendorf refilled her glass and re-lit her cigarette. She flicked ash into the green foam and said, 'What's all this fuss about Mickey, then?'

'Oh, nothing really. He is just passing through an incendiary phase.' Krippendorf sat on the still unmended bidet, holding a towel in readiness. 'He has been experimenting quite actively of late.'

Veronica moved the cigarette to one corner of her mouth with her tongue and blew out smoke from the other corner. 'He's always had that experimental streak in him,' she said. 'He gets that from my side of the family. I don't think you should discourage it.'

Krippendorf nodded abstractedly. 'He is quite well up on the general theory of combustion. It is the practical application that tends to let him down.'

'Give him a chance, he's only eleven.'

'Twelve,' he said.

'You mustn't expect too much.'

'It can be a nuisance having to keep calling the fire brigade.'

Veronica tossed her cigarette stub into the lavatory pan and said, 'What was his school report like?'

'Disappointing. In fact, almost as bad as the previous term's.'

'I've got my doubts about that place.'

'The headmaster has been on to me again. He seems convinced that Mickey would do much better somewhere else.'

'Where did he suggest?'

'He just said somewhere else.'

Veronica drained her glass in a single gulp and stood up in the bath. The green foam quickly dispersed to reveal a short, compact body with square shoulders. Against the rest of her deep tan her white breasts stood out incongruously as though they had sprouted freshly overnight. She used her hands like a rubber squeegee to remove the soap and water from her stomach and her powerful legs. As she did so she talked about her recent trip – the heat, the undrinkable water, the lack of habeas corpus. Krippendorf dried her back and patted in a desultory way at her plum-shaped buttocks.

'Is Shelley still into that Hare Krishna thing?' she asked. 'I didn't hear her chanting this morning.'

'She is with the Young Conservatives now.' He was on his knees, drying the backs of her legs. Her thighs reminded him of an old man frowning.

Veronica unpinned her thick auburn hair. It fell down her back and over her breasts and had a faintly chemical smell. 'Shouldn't you be getting dinner?' she said.

'It will not take long.'

She rubbed talcum powder over her flat stomach and into her crotch, transforming her bright auburn bush into a dull battleship grey. 'Are you trying that recipe I gave you?' she asked expectantly.

He shook his head. It was one of those dishes that called for strips of pork fat to be sewn into shanks of venison that had been marinaded in goat's milk and fenugreek. 'I thought we could have tinned ravioli and oven chips.'

Veronica groaned. 'That's wonderful. What are we drinking with it, Ribena?' She was inspecting her breasts in the bathroom mirror, lifting up the undersides with cupped hands.

'You know what the children are like,' he said. 'They hate home cooking.'

'Jamie, you've got to get them used to it. I don't intend to spend the next ten years on a diet of eggburgers and spaghetti hoops.' She wrapped herself in a white cotton robe that she had brought back from Abu Dhabi or Nepal and went into the bedroom. Krippendorf emptied the bath, cleaned it with the new trial-offer non-scratch cleaning liquid, and mopped the water off the floor. Then he went downstairs to pre-heat the oven.

The children sat motionless around the dining-table, their knives and forks held suspended above their plates as though caught in a game of musical statues. Their eyes were fixed upon the television screen where a man in a fluorescent suit was urging an elderly couple to crawl backwards through a row of inflated rubber hoops while being sprayed with chocolate foam.

'*Must* we have that thing on while we're eating?' Veronica said. She addressed by name each of her three children in turn, none of whom made any discernible response. She banged on the table with a serving spoon, upsetting the gravy-boat that Mickey had carefully balanced on the salt cellar. Finally she rose from her chair at the head of the table and wrenched the television plug from its socket. The children's faces assumed a look of shocked disbelief and they continued to stare at the blank screen for several seconds before letting out a collective shriek of protest.

'That's my favourite programme,' said Shelley, still stunned by the enormity of her mother's action.

'Second favourite, surely?' said Krippendorf genially. 'Your first favourite is the comedy series about the blind paraplegic social worker in Harlem.' He shook tomato ketchup over his instant mash.

'You shouldn't let them watch all that rubbish, Jamie,' Veronica said. 'It'll rot their minds.'

'It's better than that crap you make.' Shelley said sulkily.

'Men wearing dark glasses and waving guns about just to show off.' She pushed her plate away.

'Shelley, that is a *very* foolish and uninformed thing to say,' said Veronica. She reminded her daughter of the recent documentary she had made about lepers in Calcutta, and an earlier one about the misappopriation of earthquake funds.

'That's what I mean,' Shelley said. 'It's always that kind of stuff.'

'What kind of stuff?' Veronica spoke with menacing self-control.

'Why is it always about the rotten things that happen and never the good things?'

'It so happens that the world is a rather nasty place. I have to report things as they are, not as I'd like them to be.' She poured herself another glass of red wine, drank half of it, and refilled her glass.

'You could make cartoons,' volunteered Edmund, coughing through a mouthful of unchewed food. Observing his younger son engaged in the act of eating caused Krippendorf to wonder again if there was some impairment of co-ordination between hand and brain. He transferred food mechanically from his plate to his mouth at a much faster rate than he could chew and swallow it, so that the entire operation broke down at predictable intervals while the backlog was cleared in a choking fit. One reason why Edmund was so thin, he conjectured, was that although a great quantity of food got as far as his mouth it proved merely to be in transit to various other external destinations. The currently favoured destinations appeared to be his Tottenham Hotspur tee-shirt and Krippendorf's own plate.

'We had the TV cameras at school last week,' said Mickey. 'They came to film the riots.' He was carving an artistic design in the table with his fork. 'They ran out of film in the middle and asked us to start again.' He had large blue eyes that were a little too far apart, making his snub nose appear stranded on his face. Like his mother he had thick auburn hair, but unlike his mother's it rose into a high mound at the crown and then descended abruptly in a series of ragged steps where Krippendorf had tried to trim it with the secateurs.

After the dishes had been cleared away Veronica suggested a walk across the common. The children groaned in unison. Their mother chivvied them into their cagoules and anoraks and ushered them out into the damp evening air. 'For God's sake, it's only to the ponds and back. It's not a death march.'

They made their way along the hypotenuse of worn grass and battered shrubbery that the local residents referred to as The Square. Some of the tall terraced houses had coach-lamps at the side of the door and some had white window-shutters for protection against the fierce North London sun. Most of them had the front curtains open to reveal Afghan carpets and educational toys on sanded floors. Krippendorf knew very few of the inhabitants but assumed them to have roughly identical moral beliefs and duvet covers. He walked with long purposeful strides, avoiding the dogshit on the pavement.

They crossed the main road and went down a side turning consisting solely of Pakistani grocers, Chinese take-aways and Turkish kebab houses. Knots of teenagers stood about in the doorways eating things from polystyrene boxes and spitting Coca-Cola at each other. Beyond the side street the road inclined steeply to the common.

'Where's Mickey?' Veronica asked for the third time. They had last seen him running ahead and peering into the windows of parked cars. Edmund had one foot on the kerb and one foot in the gutter. He was kicking the empty beer-can that he had been systematically kicking since they left the house.

Shelley was deliberately lagging behind, showing her silent displeasure at having to be part of this convivial family outing. Beneath her yellow anorak she was wearing a grey dustbin liner tied around the middle with a length of washing line.

'I worry about that girl sometimes,' Veronica said, glancing over her shoulder. 'She's become so aggressive lately.'

'Hm,' Krippendorf said, adjusting his pace. He always found it difficult to synchronize his long loping strides with his wife's short quick ones.

'She's never got a civil word to say to me,' said Veronica, scurrying alongside him. 'Now that she's fourteen . . .'

'Thirteen.'

'. . . I thought I'd have a chat with her about birth control, give her some advice. Do you know what she said to me?'

Krippendorf waited to be told.

'Jamie, are you listening?'

'What did she say to you?'

'She called me a bossy old cow and said it was none of my business. Christ, I only wanted to have a motherly chat.'

On the common, people were running about with dogs and balls and shouting unnecessarily. Despite the chill breeze a queue had formed alongside the van selling soft ice-cream.

Krippendorf said, 'She told me that she had already decided in favour of the coil. She seems to have weighed the various alternatives with exemplary thoroughness.'

'Jamie, I think you might have persuaded her to discuss it with me first. It is, after all, something I *do* know about.'

'Apparently most of her friends are on the coil. They are understandably anxious not to get pregnant before their O-levels.'

Veronica swore effusively as she stumbled on the muddy grass. One of her high-heels had got stuck and she held on to him as to a lamp-post or a wall while she fitted it back on. They picked their way carefully down the grassy slope to the adventure playground and sat on a vandalized bench watching Edmund and Mickey rolling in the mud and hanging from high scaffolding by their feet.

The light was rapidly fading. Immediately overhead the sky was a mottled grey, but in the distance it was a lighter colour edged with deep blue giving way to a washed-out pink. Gradually the pink grew brighter, lighting up the entire horizon. It reminded Krippendorf of a cheap painting intended to represent a future prospect of unparalleled goodness, hope and joy.

Veronica called across to Shelley, who was sitting on a children's swing but not swinging. 'Look, isn't it marvellous, the colours.'

'What?'

'The sky,' Veronica explained, pointing at the sky. 'It's magnificent.'

Shelley pulled down the corners of her mouth. 'It's only a sunset. There's no need to have an orgasm.'

They returned the way they had come, climbing crab-like up the muddy slope. The chill breeze had developed into a cold wind and they shivered inside their waterproof clothing.

'Where's Mickey?' Veronica asked.

'I imagine he will turn up. He generally does.' Krippendorf pushed his fists deep into his pockets.

'Edmund, where's Mickey?' Veronica persisted.

'He was on the railway track messing about with the signals.'

'Jamie, did you hear that?' She grabbed his arm.

'Yes, it is so like him. He never plays with his own train set.'

They found him at the front of the queue for soft ice-cream. He was buying a triple strawberry cornet with chocolate flakes and banana fudge topping.

'Where did you get the money?' asked Edmund enviously.

'On the empty bottles.'

'Give us a lick,' said Edmund, his mouth already open in preparation.

'What empty bottles?' Krippendorf enquired.

'The Guinness bottles. I took them to the off-licence after school.'

'Mickey, they were all full bottles. I bought them for Mrs O'Shea, as partial compensation for the damage to her cat.'

His son backed quickly away. 'You can still give her the beer, I emptied the bottles into the bucket under the sink. It's all right,' he called over his shoulder, 'I washed it out with disinfectant first.'

Edmund demanded an ice-cream and then persuaded them to stop at the Tandoori take-away for a box of chicken pieces. He ate them by pushing his face inside the box. When he had finished he threw the bones in the corporation flower bed.

Krippendorf quickened his stride, anxious to get the children off to bed before the start of the disaster movie. As they were passing the church the clock struck erratically, its faint tones carried away by the wind.

'Jamie,' Veronica said breathlessly, 'will you *please* slow down. I don't like having to trot behind you like an Arab fishwife.'

'Hng,' said Krippendorf.

Two

The morning mail lay fanwise on the doormat as though it had been dealt for a hand of whist. Most of the letters, including the bills, were for Veronica, but there were two addressed to Krippendorf. One was a threatening letter from the Junior Library demanding the immediate return of *One Hundred Things To Do with a Piece of String on a Rainy Day*. The other bore a Cambridge postmark. He felt a tremor of apprehension as he turned the envelope over to reveal the black and green crest of the Malinowski Research Institute. He climbed heavily up the stairs to his study, locked the door behind him, and slit open the envelope with the handle of his coffee spoon.

Dear Dr Krippendorf,

I am writing to you once again in connection with your research project (Mal 8051/Kr) entitled 'The Hegemony of Myth: Social and Symbolic Reproduction among the Shelmikedmu of the Upper Amazon Basin'. Our records show that you completed the field-work for this study over two years ago. You were granted an extension of three months because of your illness and a further four months because of 'family disturbances'. Allowing for these extensions your Final Research Report should have been submitted on 30 June last year. It is now more than nine months overdue.

The research grant awarded you totalled £14,800,

and you are required to account for the expenditure of all monies under the follow headings: (i) Air and sea travel; (ii) Interior travel, including porterage; (iii) Tropical clothing and equipment; (iv) Medical supplies, excluding local herbal remedies; (v) Subsistence; (vi) Reimbursement of informants. Receipts should be appended in all cases.

Your research report will, in the usual way, be sent to two external assessors for their specialist opinion before finally being considered by the Scholarship and Scrutiny Committee. The Committee next convenes on 31 May, and I look forward to having your report (10 copies) to lay before it in early course.

> Yours sincerely,
> J. H. R. Wayneflete-Smith,
> Director and Emeritus Professor of
> Structural Anthropology.

Krippendorf read the letter through several times, feeling the fine quality paper with the edge of his thumbnail. Was it really £14,800, he wondered. He unlocked the drawer of his desk and took out a Building Society share book. It showed a total of £403. It was extraordinary how quickly the money had gone. He did some rough calculations on his blotting pad. There was, of course, the new Volvo; and three months in the 'villa' on Spetse. And then the loft conversion. And Shelley's elocution lessons. It all mounted up.

He took out his manuscript and thumbed through it, reading random passages with a detached and critical eye. Once again his insights and observations struck him as being surprisingly sharp, as though they had been written by somebody else. As he read on he was filled with a growing sense of optimism and self-confidence in his abilities. The more he thought about it the more certain he felt that he could give value for money by producing as good a piece of fieldwork as he might have done if he had actually gone there to do it. In some respects he might even be able to create a work of greater originality and insight than would be possible for somebody on the spot. Familiarity gave rise to its own peculiar blindness. In any case, anthropology was an unusual science. It was a well-known fact that if two anthropologists of different schools were to study the same tribe they would come up with two entirely different and contradictory accounts. If actually being in the place and witnessing things at first hand led to such confusion there was a sound case to be made for keeping one's social distance. Greatly encouraged by this line of thought and its promising ramifications he went downstairs for his fried breakfast.

After he had washed and dried the dishes he watered Veronica's indoor plants and scraped Polyfilla in the holes in the living-room wall caused by Mickey's airgun practice. Shortly after ten o'clock he put on his coat and left the house.

The sun was trying unsuccessfully to break through the clouds. Now and then it glowed weakly behind a thin patch of grey before being quickly cloaked by a thicker patch of grey. He ambled across the 'square', giving a wide berth to the small children tearing at the torn shrubbery and rolling about in the uncut grass and the dogshit. Outside every house stood jumbled heaps of black plastic garbage bags, their contents spilling onto the pavement. The dustmen's strike was in its fifth week and there was everywhere a faintly Neapolitan smell.

The high street was unusually quiet for mid-morning. Several of the shops were boarded up and some had defiant signs across the smashed windows saying 'Business as Usual'. The betting shop had been completely gutted and the doner kebab house was still smouldering. Policemen stood in twos and threes on the street corners. They had fresh young faces, curiously pink, like the faces of toy policemen. They were in good humour, smiling at the passers-by and laughing into their walkie-talkies. Krippendorf felt reassured by their presence. He was certain that he could ask any one of them the time of day or the way to the nearest bank without being clubbed. In his decent brogues and carefully knotted regimental tie they might even address him as Sir.

A slowly-moving queue wound its way around two sides of the prefabricated Social Security building. Krippendorf joined the end of it, nodding with formality to the one or two faces he recognized. He folded the back page of *The Times* into a neat rectangle and started on the crossword. Before he had unravelled the first anagram he was joined by a seemingly old man wearing an army greatcoat with no buttons.

'All right then, Captain?' the man said. He had his hands in his pockets and flapped his open coat about as though it were a pair of wings. 'Right old caper.'

Krippendorf concentrated on the clue to seven across: 'Apples not quite ripe enough to forestall unlawful participation in expurgated Welsh drama? (8,4)'

The man in the greatcoat nudged him gently. 'They got vacancies in the pickling factory,' he said in a confidential tone. 'Nice little number.'

Krippendorf shook his head sadly. 'Alas, I have very little experience of the pickling profession.' They shuffled slowly forward. 'What about yourself?' he added. 'Are you comtemplating a career in that direction?'

The man laughed. He had huge yellow teeth stripped of gum. 'I should cocoa.' He dipped at the knees and flapped his greatcoat energetically.

Krippendorf pencilled in the answer to fifteen down, an easily identifiable quotation from *Coriolanus*. He managed to complete two more clues before his companion nudged him and said, 'What exactly is your line, Captain? Strictly speaking.'

Krippendorf sucked in his breath between pursed lips and let it slowly out. He said, 'Applied hermeneutics would perhaps be the least misleading description, though the interpretation of all forms of symbolic and ritual behaviour fall within my purview, whether in a literate or pre-literate context.'

The man nodded knowingly and again dipped at the knees. 'Not much call for that round this way,' he said. 'Strictly speaking.'

There was a sudden flurry of activity and they moved forward three paces at once. Half an hour later they had reached the inside of the building. Long fluorescent lamps glowed above the hardboard partitions and the long rows of steel filing cabinets. There was a powerful sense of dust falling through the air, although no dust was immediately visible.

'Name?' said the woman behind the counter without looking up.

He told her twice and then spelled it letter by letter in the military manner. She looked at him carefully and riffled through a dog-eared file in search of disqualifying evidence.

'Sign here.' She had a smile like a tin-opener.

Krippendorf disdainfully rejected the proferred ball-point in favour of his fountain pen and its rich brown ink and made his signature with an elaborate flourish. He folded the giro cheque in two and placed it carefully in his wallet while the woman watched. He nodded courteously and made his way out, first pausing to drop a coin into the collection box for the victims of the mortgage riots.

In the high street he was approached by a young man with a clipboard. 'Sign the petition?' he asked, smiling through his ginger beard.

Krippendorf stared with unconcealed distaste at the young man's red neckerchief and anti-nuclear badges.

'It's about the deportation of the TUC.' He advanced his

clipboard. It had a pencil attached to it by a piece of furry string.

'For or against?' Krippendorf enquired.

'Against, of course, sign here.'

'Certainly not.' Krippendorf walked briskly away and crossed the road by the looted ironmongers to avoid passing directly in front of the Co-op.

The sky was still overcast after a night of drizzle, though the deep depression moving from the west was predicted to give way later to bright periods followed by thundery showers and strong easterly winds rising to gale force in the north. Krippendorf decided to ignore the few flecks of rain as he hung the morning washing on the line. There were never enough pegs to go round and he found himself having to tie the shirts to the line by their sleeves. Several of them had buttons missing down the front where he had crushed them with the steam iron.

'Doing your washing, then, Mr K.?' The top half of Mrs O'Shea's face appeared just above the fence in its customary place. She had something woollen on her head that looked as if it must have fallen there without her knowledge.

'Not really,' he said. 'I have already done the washing. I am now proceeding with the drying. Though as a matter of fact I expect the wind rather than myself to be the principal agent in that regard.' He tied Edmund's blue-and-white-striped sock around the line in a granny knot. There was only one sock that colour.

'They'll never dry properly like that,' advised Mrs O'Shea. She adjusted her grip on the low fence, thereby reinforcing the impression that she was balancing on tiptoe. It occurred to him that he very rarely saw the rest of her, although he knew that she had the kind of legs that grew progressively thicker from knee to ankle so that her ankles overlapped the sides of her shoes.

'I do not believe in completely dry socks,' he said. 'Especially for children. Children's socks should always tend towards dampness. It retards the natural growth of the feet, which in turn makes for considerable economy on shoes.' He shook the fluff off Veronica's scarlet kaftan and knotted it to the line. He did the same with her white embroidered blouse, noticing as he did so that it had turned a curiously streaky pink.

'By the way, Mr K., I was wondering if I could have a quick word with you.' With visible effort she had managed to get her chin above the fence.

'Now is not the best time for me, Mrs O'Shea. I have to get the fish fingers on.'

'It's about your Mickey.'

'I imagined it might be.' He stuffed the two remaining odd socks in his pocket and hurried to the back door.

'He keeps putting notes in my milk bottle.'

'I shall take the matter up with him.' He closed the door behind him.

'The milkman left me twenty-seven pints this morning.'

On Saturday afternoon he took the children shopping for new clothes. Throughout the bus ride to the West End they complained bitterly about having to spend three consecutive hours away from the television set. Each time the bus passed an electrical goods shop they craned their necks to catch a fleeting glimpse of the flickering screens in the window.

'Look, the wrestling's on,' Edmund whined.

'And the snooker,' Mickey said, pushing his penknife into the seat and twisting the blade experimentally.

Shelley said, 'There's a film I wanted to watch on BBC 2

about runaway nuns.' Her bare legs were dangling over the back of the seat in front.

'You wouldn't have been able to watch it anyway,' Edmund said.

'Why not?'

'Because we'd have had the wrestling on, stupid.'

'Snooker,' insisted Mickey.

'Not if I'd switched the film on first,' Shelley said. 'You can't change channels if someone's already watching something. That's the rule, isn't it, Jim-Jam?'

Krippendorf grunted absent-mindedly as he searched his pockets for the shopping list.

'Oh no,' Mickey protested, 'that's the rule only if there's a clash between children's programmes and grown-ups' programmes. Mum made that rule so she could watch the wildlife programme instead of Benny Hill.'

Shelley turned to him fiercely. 'Well the film I wanted to see is a grown-ups' film, so the same rule applies.'

'No it doesn't,' Mickey said heatedly. 'You're not a grown-up. What counts is whether you're a grown-up or a child, not what the programme is.'

'Don't be so thick,' Shelley yelled. 'Of course it's the programme that counts.'

Passengers in the front of the bus were turning in their seats to stare.

'Bollocks,' Mickey shouted. 'It's a children's programme if it's children who want to watch it, even if it was really made for grown-ups.'

'Don't talk crap.'

'I'm not talking crap. Benny Hill was counted as a children's programme because we were the ones who wanted to watch it. It's really meant for grown-ups.'

'No it isn't,' Shelley hissed.

'Yes it bloody is. That's why it's full of bums and tits.'

They continued to argue violently about which of the several hypothetically possible programmes they would now in fact be watching on the assumption that they were seated in front of a television screen instead of on the upper deck of a number fourteen bus.

'Try and be a little quieter,' Krippendorf said, still turning out his pockets. 'If there is any further quarrelling about television I shall forbid you to watch the midnight horror movie.'

They lapsed into a moody silence, but not before Shelley had put in the last word. 'Anyway,' she muttered, 'it was Mummy's silly rule, and since she's hardly ever home it doesn't count.'

They bought jeans in a dimly lit basement that shook with music, and underwear from a man selling furtively from a suitcase. Mickey wanted a leather belt with a heavy metal buckle and Shelley wanted white leather boots that she could paint a different colour. Edmund asked only for things to put in his mouth. They shambled through the crowds in Regent's Street and Carnaby Street, each of them trailing a lurid plastic carrier. At Oxford Circus they found the road cordoned off because of a bomb scare. They made their way to Selfridges through the back streets, squeezing their way past stationary ambulances, fire engines and police cars.

In Selfridges he lost them. After twenty minutes' fruitless search he took the lift to the top floor and worked his way down floor by floor. He found them in the basement, each squatting in front of a different television set watching a different programme. He managed to get them away only after deploying the usual combination of imprecations, ultimata, entreaties and supplications.

They went home by Underground. Mickey wriggled under the ticket barrier and ran all the way down the up escalator. In the carriage, Edmund swung gibbon-like from strap-handle to strap-handle without touching the floor with his feet. In the process he kicked Shelley in the neck and she immediately retaliated with one of her new leather boots.

Krippendorf observed his children's behaviour in public places with professional interest. Their actions did not appear to conform to any recognizable norms of social behaviour, yet they were too consistent and predictable to be classified as random. There must be some hidden pattern underlying the apparent chaos, some implicit logic which could render their behaviour perfectly intelligible. He took a pencil and notebook from his pocket and recorded the order and frequency with which they punched, bit and gouged one another, and the approximate ratio of physical to verbal assaults. Gradually an idea began to take shape in his mind. He closed his eyes and let it unfold of its own accord as the train rattled and swayed through its narrow black hole.

As soon as they got home he went straight to his study, locked the door behind him, and began to write.

Chapter Four:
Savagery and Socialization in Amazonia

Among the Shelmikedmu child-rearing and the social-ization of the young are the sole responsibility of fathers. Even new-born babies are weaned exclusively by men. It is an everyday sight in the village to see a young father warming coconut milk on the fire and feeding it to his infant through a bamboo tube with a softened tip. Fermented palm sap is generally mixed with the milk as a soporific. Shelmikedmu babies are seldom heard to cry or even seen awake other than at feeding time.

From about the age of nine months infants are wrapped in banana-leaf swaddling and carried strapped to their father's thigh with strips of bark. This is done to prevent the infants from crawling around the hut and disturbing the carefully preserved interior order (see Chapter Two). When they reach an age at which they are too heavy or awkward to carry they are tethered to a post well away from the hut. One common way of settling scores with an errant neighbour is to cut his child loose at a well-chosen moment, allowing it to run amok among the pots and pans. When they get too big to be swaddled or tethered, children pose more serious problems of social control. Fathers then enforce a strict code of conduct designed to reduce all contact between adults and children to the barest minimum. Shelmikedmu believe that children are the natural prey of malignant spirits. These spirits normally enter the child's body through its mouth whenever adults are present. Consequently, children are required to keep their mouths tightly shut whenever they are in the company of men. Those who break this rule have their mouths stuffed with rancid cassava pulp and bound closed with strips of reed. This treatment is known to kill off the possessing spirit and free the child from its evil grip.

Apart from maintaining total silence in the presence of adults, children are expected to show the utmost deference and courtesy to their fathers at all times. Boys and girls are required to keep their heads bowed whenever their father is present. Each evening they must bathe his feet, de-louse his hair, and rub his body with warm alligator fat. I observed that the children carried out these duties with obvious relish, such is the esteem and respect in which their fathers are held.

Shelmikedmu children, as a result of their upbringing, rarely quarrel among themselves. They share all their small possessions with one another freely and gladly. They are unerringly gracious, considerate and polite to each other in all circumstances. During my entire stay I witnessed only one outburst of fractious behaviour – when the small son of a village headman slapped his sister on the knee with her blowpipe. He

35

was immediately punished in the traditional manner by having his penis-sheath filled with soldier ants.

Children's unquestioning obedience to their fathers' every wish, and their harmonious relations with each other, are especially noticeable on . . .

He was interrupted in his flow by a shuddering crash from somewhere below, as though the refrigerator had been flung into the bath. Then a door banged, followed by a sound akin to a rugby team racing drunkenly up and down the stairs. He unlocked the study door and put his head out. 'What exactly is happening down there?' he called.

Shelley was on the way up to her room. 'It's only Mickey,' she said. 'He's trying to flush Edmund down the toilet.'

'Will you please tell him to stop. I have only just cleaned it.'

'Tell him yourself,' she said, and slammed her bedroom door behind her.

He hurried down to the bathroom where he found Mickey mopping at Edmund's red eyes and dripping head with a wad of lavatory paper.

'He pushed my face down the lav and pulled the chain,' Edmund sobbed. His normally curly hair was now plastered flat across his forehead.

'It was only a game,' Mickey said.

'Game? What kind of game?' Krippendorf wrapped a towel around Edmund's head to make a turban.

'We were playing political prisoners. I was trying to make him confess.' Mickey's wide blue eyes blinked uncomprehendingly at all the fuss.

'It's not fair,' Edmund choked, 'I'm always the prisoner and he's always the policeman. We should take it in turns.'

Krippendorf ushered them both out of the bathroom. 'Try to find a quieter way of extracting confessions,' he said. 'You are disturbing my research.'

Mickey's face suddenly lit up. 'What about electricity?' he said. 'That's quiet. That's what they all use now. We could strip the wires from your Black and Decker.'

'Certainly not,' his father ruled. 'No electricity. It is far too costly, we are only on the domestic tariff.' He ran the towel around the bathroom floor with his foot and then returned to the tranquillity of his study and the manageable world of Amazonia.

The telephone rang while he was trying to extract the giblets from a frozen chicken. He was gripping it between his knees and hitting it with a screwdriver. He snatched up the receiver and said, 'Veronica Yardley is not at home, pip, pip, pip. She is expected back from Uttar Pradesh on Tuesday, pip, pip, pip. If you wish to leave a message, please speak now, pip, pip, pip.'

'Dr Krippendorf?'

'Yes?' He relaxed his grip on the frozen chicken.

'You don't know me, my name's Dunkerley. I've been put on to you by the Malinowski Research Institute.'

'Oh.' He felt his heart change gear.

'I understand from one of the typists there that you're a leading authority on the tribes of Amazonia.'

'Not all of them. Just one, actually.'

'It's the one you know about that I'm really interested in. My typist friend tells me they're a fascinating bunch, lots of funny customs. She enjoys reading your preliminary reports. I forget what they're called now – Shellimoco? Shammacadam?'

Krippendorf looked into the mouthpiece. 'What exactly is it that you want?' he said coldly.

'I'm just coming to that. The thing is, old boy, I've just taken over the editorship of the *British Journal of Structural Anthropology*. I'd very much like you to write a piece for us.'

'Aha.'

'Nothing too technical or high falutin'. Something simple and punchy, d'you know what I mean?'

'I am not sure that I do.'

'Well, the fact of the matter is, old boy, I intend to give the old *Journal* a bit of a face-lift. It's far too dull and stodgy. It's full of scientific jargon and theoretical mumbo-jumbo that only a handful of people can understand.'

'Anthropologists, you mean?'

'Exactly. What I want to do is to give it a much broader appeal, make it more accessible to ordinary people. You'd be surprised, there's an enormous popular interest in anthropology that simply isn't being catered for.'

'I had no idea.'

'I'm absolutely sure we can build a mass circulation if we brighten the thing up and market it properly. I want to see it sold in the high street newsagents among the leisure mags. I want to make it available at railway station bookstalls and at the supermarket checkout. We could run competitions and talent contests. We could organize cultural trips to places of anthropological interest. The possibilities are enormous.'

'Hm.' Krippendorf set the chicken down on the floor and eased the damp patch on his trouser leg away from his skin.

'The first thing I intend to do,' Dunkerley continued, 'is to change the name. As from next month it'll be called *Exotica*. It's going to be in colour and sold at half the present price. I know it's going to go like a bomb.' He went on to reveal his plans for a mass advertising compaign on Channel Four and a spectacular publicity drive culminating in the distribution of free copies by Zulu warriors in Trafalgar Square.

'Now, what I was wondering, old boy, is whether you could do me two thousand words on clitorectomy?'

'The Shelmikedmu do not practise clitorectomy.' At

least, he reflected, they have not until now. It was a custom they might readily adopt.

'What about incest, then? Or cannibalism? Or infanticide? Anything that would be of interest to the intelligent layman.'

Krippendorf pursed his lips thoughtfully. 'I believe I do have something on the stocks that might be pertinent. I should need a little time to polish it up.'

'We'd pay quite generously. That's all part of the new policy.'

Krippendorf's face took on a pained expression. 'The question of remuneration is unimportant. What matters is that scientific knowledge should be made public. I am quite prepared to make my own small contribution to that end.'

'That's the spirit, old boy,' Dunkerley said. 'Could you let me have your piece by Friday week?'

'So soon?'

'Afraid so, old boy, if it's to make the first issue. I'd like to get the thing off with a bang.'

He talked enthusiastically about the other articles he had commissioned for the launch: a piece on bride capture among the Nuer; the confessions of a defrocked missionary priest; drug addiction among the Hopi. Before ringing off he said, 'One more thing. I assume you have photographs of this tribe of yours? Our new readers are likely to be more interested in the pictures than the text.'

'Of course,' Krippendorf said without thinking.

'In colour?'

'Naturally.'

'Jolly good, old boy. I'm looking forward to seeing them.'

Whistling his high-pitched tuneless whistle he went from room to room gathering up Veronica's rubber plants and assembling them in a shaded corner of the garden. First he carefully removed the *Ficus elastica decora* from its expensive earthenware pot and transplanted it in the previously prepared patch of soil next to the failed marrow bed. He did the same with the tall *Ficus pandurata* and the stunted *F. bengalensis*. Finally he transplanted the luxuriant yucca and the small cacti that normally gathered dust on Shelley's mantelpiece. In front of the plants he arranged a frayed strip of coconut matting and a few bits of discoloured raffia.

He stood back to survey the general effect, dropping on one knee and squinting through the aperture made by his thumb and middle finger. It was really quite convincing, he thought, though the sooty hawthorn bush did not look altogether right as the backdrop. The prints could always be touched up afterwards. He busied himself for a few more minutes picking up sweet wrappers and bottle-tops before going up to the bathroom to supervise the progress of his sons.

They were squatting naked in the empty bath, coating one another with reddish-brown theatrical greasepaint.

'This stuff pongs,' Mickey complained as he squeezed the tube across his brother's pigeon chest. Edmund was wiping something from his eye with a face flannel. 'Will this black dye wash out of our hair?' he asked.

'It will eventually,' Krippendorf assured him. 'Though actually it rather suits you.'

Mickey stood up in the bath and began rubbing greasepaint across his stomach and thighs. 'Must I do my balls too?' he enquired. 'And my maggot?'

'Everything. Be as quick as you can, the light will be fading soon.'

Edmund steadied himself with one hand and massaged greasepaint into his almost fleshless buttocks with the other. 'Dad, why have we got to do this?' he asked plaintively.

'I have already told you. It is to do with my scientific research. I thought you would appreciate the opportunity to take part in a cultural experiment.'

40

'As well as having new roller skates,' Mickey quickly reminded him.

'Only if you do it properly.'

'Imported ones, not British.'

'Obviously.'

Edmund said, 'I don't really want roller skates. I'd rather have the money instead.'

'Anything you wish, so long as you hurry. I do not want to have to use flash.'

When their skin had been darkened to his satisfaction he wrapped them each in a bath towel and hurried them into the garden. After much badgering and cajoling he managed to get them to adopt a kneeling position in front of the rubber plants. He removed their towels and hung around their necks a double string of wooden beads he had bought at the ethnic jumble sale. Then he painted white diagonal stripes across their cheeks with Tipp-Ex fluid. Finally, he fetched from the garden shed a large firelog with two flat surfaces and placed it directly in front of Edmund.

'Now, kneel right up to the log, as close as you can get.'

'What for?'

'Just do it.'

Edmund pressed himself against the log.

'Good. Now lay your maggot on the surface. And try not to let the foreskin slip back.'

'Why?'

'Stop asking silly questions.'

Krippendorf took from his pocket a shard of flintstone that had been fashioned into a crude cutting instrument. 'Mickey, you take this and hold it three or four inches above Edmund's maggot.'

Mickey's wide eyes glistened in anticipation, and Edmund let out a shriek of alarm as his brother feigned a violent chopping motion with the stone instrument.

'Could we please have less frivolity,' Krippendorf said.

'This is a solemn ceremony.' He was fiddling about with the camera, adjusting the focus, checking the light meter. He peered through the viewfinder and shifted his position to avoid incorporating the side of the garden shed and the sheet of rusted corrugated iron by the hawthorn bush.

'Hurry up, Dad, I'm getting goose pimples,' Edmund whined.

'Absolutely still,' Krippendorf said. 'Mickey, do not make that ridiculous face.' He crawled about taking pictures from different angles and experimenting with variations on the basic pose. He had already written the first draft of the accompanying text.

Circumcision Rites among the Shelmikedmu

Shelmikedmu boys are not usually circumcised until they have reached the age of six or seven. The tribal elders say that if the operation is carried out when the child is younger his penis will cease to grow. They point out that this frequently happens among the white man.

The responsibility for performing this ritual falls on the shoulders of the initiate's elder brother or cousin. As may be seen from the photograph, the brother of the initiate is himself quite young, a fact consistent with the Shelmikedmu emphasis on encouraging early maturity.

Fathers are never entrusted with this task for the simple reason that sons are regarded as legitimate competitors for the sexual favours of their father's wives. My informants told me that in earlier times fathers did perform the operation on their sons, but that the practice was discontinued after a series of unexplained mishaps.

Once the skin has been removed it is generally sold to a medicine man who hangs it in the sun to dry.

When it has thoroughly seasoned it is crushed into a fine powder and mixed with anaconda droppings and smoked in clay pipes as a cure for impotence.

'Excuse me asking, Mr K., but is everything all right?' Mrs O'Shea's face floated above the fence. She watched with open mouth as Mickey and Edmund cavorted about naked on the coconut matting, ullulating inappropriately in the manner of Hollywood Apaches.

'What's happened to them?' she said. 'Why have they gone that colour?'

Krippendorf wound on the film and returned the camera to its case. 'The doctors cannot explain it,' he said. 'They have advised me to call in the vet.'

'Oh my God.'

'Let us hope they do not have to be put down.'

They drove through the quiet Sunday streets in the direction of Highgate. A warm breeze rustled the leaves of the cankered plane trees, but was not quite strong enough to scatter the old newspapers and hamburger wrappers that accumulated in the gutters awaiting settlement of the roadsweepers' redundancy dispute. Veronica sat bolt upright behind the steering wheel, one hand permanently on the gear lever. She drove in short, sharp bursts, racing towards road junctions and traffic lights and then braking suddenly. Krippendorf allowed his body to lurch back and forth in its seat in silent commentary.

'Will there be food there?' Edmund asked, his pale triangular face creased in anxiety.

'Jessie always puts on a lovely spread,' said Veronica. 'She gets it all from Fortnum's.'

'It won't be those little things on sticks, will it? Or bits of food on tiny biscuits?'

'For heaven's sake, child, you've just eaten two huge breakfasts.'

'That was ages ago.' He pushed his fist into a jumbo packet of smoky bacon crisps and spread the contents around his mouth.

Veronica jolted the car to a halt at a zebra crossing. A woman wrapped in furs led what appeared to be a large woolly rat across the road on a leash. When it reached the kerb the animal turned around in circles before establishing itself in a shitting position. The woman held the leash at arm's length and stared into the far distance with great intensity.

At the bottom of Highgate Hill they were held up by a procession. A straggling group of marchers were on their way to join a larger demonstration. Some of them carried furled banners and others were holding neatly printed placards stapled on to poles. They were flanked on either side by embarrassed policemen.

'Is is Ban the Bomb?' Edmund spluttered through a mouthful of crisps.

'Of course it isn't, stupid,' Mickey informed him. 'It's about putting the unions in prison.'

'Why do they want to put them in prison?'

Mickey groaned. 'They're already in prison, dumbo. They want them let out again.'

'Well why are they in?'

'Because they asked for too much money, the greedy pigs,' said Shelley. 'It serves them right.' She dilated her nostrils and made a small readjustment to her gunmetal nose-plug.

A few minutes later they pulled up outside a large detached house in a leafy crescent full of other equally large and detached houses. They were greeted at the front door by a spindly woman wearing a fawn trouser suit and a filigree torque around her neck.

'Darling,' she said to Veronica.

'Jessie.'

The two women embraced and kissed each other notionally on the cheek like Russian diplomats on an airport runway. Krippendorf held out his hand but Jessie thrust her chin at him, partially closing her eyes.

'James,' she said, clasping him loosely by the wrists. 'You're looking terribly suave.' She looked him up and down, purporting to admire his new mustard-coloured hacking jacket and purple cravat. 'I can see Veronica's been taking you shopping.' Krippendorf said nothing but smiled in a way that could have been interpreted as either confirmation or denial. Jessie led them through the house to the garden at the rear. People were sitting about in small groups on the lawn and talking over their drinks in the animated way of people who see each other every day at work. They were mostly friends of Veronica from the television studios, several of whom Krippendorf thought he recognized. For some reason they were all called Mo, Di, Al, Bo, Jo or Cy. He accepted a glass of chilled hock offered to him on a tray by a total stranger and sat uncomfortably on the lawn.

Veronica was standing at one end of a semi-circle of ostensibly young men dressed in safari jackets. She was talking excitedly, emphasizing her remarks by slicing the air with a succession of karate chops. Krippendorf noted the way in which she engaged the whole of her compact body in the act of conversation, as though the weight of what she had to say could never be supported by words alone.

Shelley was sitting on the wall of the ornamental fountain talking to someone he vaguely recognized – a dubbing mixer called Ed or Lou. The latter whispered something in her ear and she blushed and began fiddling distractedly with the pink laces of her surgical boots.

'Hi there.'

Krippendrof looked up to see a woman with exemplary

teeth smiling down upon him. Before he could get to his feet she had lowered herself daintily beside him, keeping her knees close together. 'D'you mind if I sit here?'

He inclined his head ambiguously. 'I am merely a guest here. I have no proprietorial rights.'

The woman tugged her skirt over her knees. She did this with one hand, trying not to spill the glass of hock in the other. She said, 'You're Vee's husband, I believe?'

He looked at her evenly. 'I think not. Whose husband?'

'Vee's. Veronica's. We all call Veronica Vee.'

'Ah.' He held his wine glass up to the light, decoding the message of its contents. 'I suppose Veronica is rather a mouthful.'

She let out a chirruping laugh. 'I've heard all about you. I've been forewarned.' In a different tone of voice she said, 'You used to be an anthropologist or archaeologist or something?'

'Used to be?'

'Oh dear, have I put my foot in it? I understood you were . . .' Her words trailed off into an apologetic mumble.

Krippendorf cleared his throat. 'I am no longer in the employ of the university, if that is what you mean. But that hardly qualifies as an impediment these days, now that they teach nothing but commercial arithmetic and fisheries science.' As he spoke he caught sight of Edmund hovering by the smoked salmon sandwiches and imported strawberries. His son suddenly darted to the trestle table, seized two sandwiches and thrust them into his mouth while simultaneously reaching for a third which he gripped in his fist as though preparing to bowl it overarm.

The woman said, 'Vee suggested I should have a word with you about the programme I'm working on. It's called Sorcery in the Suburbs. Do you mind if I pick your brains?'

Krippendorf smiled with his mouth only. 'I am not terribly well up on the suburban literature, it is rather outside my sphere of interest.' He ran the back of his hand across the recently mown grass. 'I can however tell you that Hemel Hempstead is the principal centre of suburban sorcery. I am given to understand it is rampant there among the lower classes.'

'Hemel Hempstead?'

'Yes, you can get there on a Green Line bus.'

She took a black leather notebook from her handbag and jotted something down.

He said, 'At the Nairobi conference on witchcraft and sorcery the Hemel Hempstead case was discussed at considerable length. It has many unusual features, anthropologically speaking.'

She gave a puzzled frown. 'Why Hemel Hempstead of all places?'

Krippendorf pushed out his lower lip thoughtfully. 'Causation is always a problem in the cultural sciences,' he said. 'There are some who argue that the social milieu of Hemel Hempstead is intrinsically conducive to the spread of black magic among the populace. There are, on the other hand, those who claim that the people who migrate there already have a psychosocial predisposition towards the occult. The problem gave rise to tremendous controversy at Nairobi.' He brushed dandruff off the collar of his new jacket.

'Do you mean they dress up and cast spells, and all that sort of thing?' She was busy scribbling notes with a tiny stub of pencil.

'I am not conversant with the ethnographic minutiae. You will find them all recorded in the *Oxford Journal of Supernatural Science*. I could send you the reference.' The bones in his knees cracked as he rose to his feet. 'I must ask you to excuse me now. I have not seen my son Mickey for the past half-hour. That is never a good sign.'

He ambled about the garden holding his green-stemmed glass in front of him as evidence of his right to be there. He listened for a while to a group of people discussing the respective merits of Eisenstein and Buñuel and then eavesdropped on an argument about the medicinal properties of garlic. Presently he went into the house in search of a lavatory.

It struck him once again how orderly other people's houses appeared to be. There were no obvious jam stains on the walls or lumps gouged out of the easy chairs. Nor, when walking across the room, was it necessary to kick a swathe through abandoned clothing and devastated comics. Even the bathroom, he noted, had neither puddles on the lavatory seat nor toothpaste on the shaving mirror.

On his way out he was buttonholed by a drunken Montenegrin who insisted on telling him about his recent trip to Chicago. 'I couldn't believe it,' he kept saying. 'I just couldn't believe it.' He was leaning unsteadily against the passage wall, holding his wine glass with both hands for support. 'I was at this disco, dancing with this girl. She was a lovely girl. She was like a girl you only see in the movies. She asked me where I was from and I said Titograd. Titograd? she said. Is that the place in Iowa where they have the dinosaur museum? After the dance she asked me if I liked carfee. I said I loved carfee. She said, I'll make you some at my place.

'We went back to her apartment in this building made of glass. This was in Chicago, Illinois. She disappeared for five minutes and came back wearing only her gloves and shoes. How about that? she said, turning around and around. I said to her, Where's the carfee? You invited me here for carfee. Where the fark are you from, she said, the Middle Ages?

'Do you know what happened then? Can you imagine? We were in her bedroom humping away, and in the middle of it she reaches for the phone. I must ring my husband in Princeton, New Jersey, she said. Don't stop. She talked to her husband on the phone while I was humping her. She told him everything I was doing. He's sucking my nipples,

George, she said. He's got his tongue up my ass, George, she said. I've got his cark in my hand, George, she said. It's a wonderful cark, George, it's got a head like an aubergine. I'm going to rub the phone with his cark now, George, she said, can you feel? Oh George, he's got it inside me now, he's banging away at me on our waterbed, George, she said. I'm going to come any second, George. Oh George, I'm coming right now. She gave this long groan into the phone and then put it back on the hook. I just couldn't believe it.'

He pulled at the sleeve of Krippendorf's new jacket. 'Can you believe it?' he said.

'It does seem an odd thing to do,' Krippendorf conceded. 'Particularly in view of the cost of long-distance calls.' He released himself gently from the Montenegrin's grip and went quickly into the garden.

He found Edmund by the ornamental fountain. 'I feel sick,' he said, holding his stomach and pulling a face like a sick child in a comic strip.

'Have you seen Mickey?' his father asked.

'He was trying to get on the roof.'

'What on earth for?'

'He wanted to roll the dustbins off it.'

Krippendorf scanned the surrounding rooftops for signs of his son's presence. Everything looked unnervingly normal. He searched the rhododendron bushes and went to where the dustbins were kept at the back of the house. A curious whimpering sound came from behind the sauna. He peered around it and saw Veronica. She had her back to him and was being kissed by a short man with needlessly large and hairy hands. His hands were gripping her buttocks, rotating one clockwise and the other anti-clockwise. Krippendorf wondered briefly whether this was an acquired skill before creeping away unobserved.

Shelley was still deep in conversation with Ed or Lou. She was writing something on a scrap of paper which she then handed to him, smiling foolishly. Without reading it he folded it in two and slipped it in the breast pocket of his safari jacket.

Jessie was flouncing about the garden with a bottle of Wachenheimer Mandelgarten Spatlese in each hand, topping up the glasses. He covered his own glass with his hand as she tilted a bottle towards him. 'I think I shall probably be driving,' he said. He lit a cigar and eased his long body into a rickety deck chair. The fine weather had held, but there was now a slight edge to the breeze. From somewhere in the distance came the sound of bells. All in all, he thought, it was another perfectly ordinary Sunday.

Three

On the last day of the month he received a letter from the editor of *Exotica*.

Dear Dr Krippendorf,

I have much pleasure in enclosing my cheque for £550 in respect of your illustrated article entitled 'Cognitive Dissonance and Symbolic Mediations: A Neo-Structuralist Account of Circumcision Rituals among the Shelmikedmu'. A somewhat edited and shortened version of this article has now been published in our first issue under the title 'Fantasies and Foreskins'. A complimentary copy has been despatched to you under separate cover. Please check the serial number on the back page to see whether you have won a free copy of *The Sexual Life of Savages* (unexpurgated edition).

Yours sincerely,
Alasdair Dunkerley,
Managing Editor and Cultural Adviser,
Exotica Enterprises Ltd.

Early the following week Dunkerley telephoned.

'It's all going amazingly well, old boy. Couldn't really be better. I could have sold next month's advertising space three times over.' He talked enthusiastically about his plans for a special issue on infanticide to coincide with the birth of

51

the royal baby, and his scheme to run a monthly competition of cross-cultural bingo.

'Anyway, why I'm ringing you, old boy, is for two things. Firstly, to say personally how very much I liked that piece you sent us. The photographs were terrific. We've been inundated with letters from our readers asking for more stuff on the . . . er . . . on this tribe of yours. You certainly seem to have touched a nerve.'

'It is gratifying when scholarship is appreciated,' Krippendorf said. He picked at the ancient encrustations of porridge or chewing-gum on the kitchen radiator. 'And what was the second thing?'

'What?'

'You intimated that you had two things to say, one of which you have now said.'

Dunkerley coughed into the mouthpiece. 'Well, actually, old boy, I was wondering if you'd do another piece for us. Now that the public appetite has been whetted we should try to satisfy it, right?'

Krippendorf nodded. 'I concur entirely. As a matter of fact . . .'

'Excellent.'

'. . . I do have something in draft form that I was thinking of submitting.'

'Marvellous.'

'What it is principally concerned with is kinship terminology and meta-linguistics. You see, I believe that Chomsky has got it altogether wrong. To put it another way, he is right for reasons quite different from those he mistakenly holds.' He expatiated at some length upon the intimate connection between linguistic usages and climatic conditions in Amazonia. When he had finished there was an ambiguous silence at the other end.

'Absolutely fascinating, old boy. I'm sure you're dead right. The fact is, though, that it's not exactly what I had in mind for the next issue. What I've got lined up is a special number in celebration of primitive womanhood. Young primitive womanhood, that is.'

Krippendorf twiddled with the telephone cord, straightening out its curls. 'I might be able to let you have something on female gang warfare.'

'One thing to bear in mind,' said Dunkerley, 'is that from now on the emphasis is going to be much more on the pictorial side. I don't want the pages cluttered up with too much text. Just a paragraph or two underneath each photograph, bringing out the human angle.'

'I see, I think.'

'The focal point is going to be the centrefold. I'm looking for something really eye-catching for that spot. Nothing smutty, mind you. I don't want the educational aims of the journal to get misconstrued as lewdness.'

'I should hope not.' Krippendorf said with a frown.

'Now, old boy, can you possibly help us out? Do you have any pictures of your people that would have the right kind of readership appeal?' There was a sound of paper being rustled at the other end. 'According to the market research Johnnies, our average reader is a middle-aged male unemployed heterosexual Tory voter behind with the mortgage payments on his council house.'

Krippendorf found himself ruminating aloud. 'Shelmikedmu woman are undoubtedly photogenic. Some of them are physically very striking.'

'Full frontal if possible.'

'It so happens that the female physique has an indirect but nevertheless crucial bearing upon the normative and moral order.' Even as he spoke the broad outlines of his analysis were already taking shape. Recording the details on paper would be the simplest of tasks. 'I could probably let you have an article in a matter of days,' he said brightly.

'And the photographs?'

Krippendorf was already turning over the possibilities.

'They are not immediately accessible. I should need a little longer.'

Dunkerley named a deadline and went on to talk about copyright and film royalties. 'As I see it,' he said, 'you could do wonders with this lot of yours. Really put them on the map. You could do for them what Margaret Mead did for the Trobriand Islanders. Know what I mean?'

All that morning while he ironed the sheets, scraped egg yolk off the walls and prepared the rhubarb crumble he pondered upon the problems of photography. He had in his mind a very clear image of the typical Shelmikedmu maiden; what was less clear so far was how this image was to be translated into actuality. If only Shelley were a little older, a little darker, a good deal plumper, and altogether more co-operative. His kind of anthropology, he mused, as he rubbed cooking fat into the flour, continually threw up new challenges not generally encountered by more orthodox schools. Still deep in thought, he strolled across to the Carpenters' Arms for a ploughman's lunch. Later that afternoon it suddenly came to him.

He brushed his hair, put on his flowery Jaeger shirt and matching tie and scrubbed the nap on his brown suede shoes. Shortly after three-fifteen he left the house and strode purposefully in the direction of Edmund's primary school. In the course of his short journey he was stopped on three separate occasions by beggars asking for food or money. To each of them he gave a small silver coin from the supply he carried expressly for this purpose. The beggars seemed to be getting younger and more numerous all the time. Some of them played musical instruments but mostly they stood on street corners holding out tin cups or battered hats.

He went under the dank railway bridge and crossed the strip of waste land bordering the new council estate.

Edmund's school was next to the estate. It was surrounded by high metal railings with chicken-wire stretched across the top. On one of its red brick walls was a garish mural depicting scenes of inter-racial harmony, most of which had been defaced by aerosol sprays. Young mothers chatted in twos and threes outside the gates. They were dressed in jeans or unfashionably short skirts, but several wore saris or silk pantaloons, and two were wearing yashmaks. Krippendorf exchanged pleasantries as he passed by, himself a familiar figure among the three-thirty gathering. He leaned against the vandalized telephone booth and waited for the arrival of the young Filipino woman he knew as 'Leroy's mum'.

She turned the corner as the school bell was sounding. She was pushing a canvas baby buggy containing a pillow case stuffed with laundry. He waited until she had drawn alongside. 'Hello,' he said on a note of pleasant surprise.

'Oh, hello.' She brought the buggy to a halt, causing the laundry to tip forward into Krippendorf's waiting hands. 'I thought I was going to be late again,' she said breathlessly. 'Poor little bugger had to wait twenty minutes for me yesterday. It's them buses.'

'They can be unpredictable.'

'Nearly half an hour I been waiting for the number fourteen, then three of them come at once. I gave the conductor a right mouthful.' Her hair was plaited in long braids and tied at the ends with strips of white cloth. She chatted on amiably about the scandalous price of school dinners and the transvestite headmaster. 'You letting your kid go on this trip to Didcot Power Station?' she said. 'Leroy's been nagging me about it.'

'I can think of no principled objection.'

'Ninety-five pee they're asking. I reckon they got a nerve. What they think we are, millionaires?' Her expression invited him to share her sense of mild outrage. He was impressed by the reddish-brown tint of her skin and the heavy swell beneath her striped rugby jersey. The first time he had met her he thought she must have had her arms folded beneath her woolly jumper.

Children were now rushing about the asphalt playground hitting each other with rolled-up coats and duffel bags. The young mums from the council flats were shrieking out their children's names above the din.

'Damien! Samantha! Jason!'

'Camilla! Wayne! Yvette!'

'Justin! Melissa! Darrell!'

Raising his own voice above the pandemonium, Krippendorf said, 'Edmund is having a party on Friday. He would very much like Leroy to come.'

'Oh that's nice,' she said. 'I was going to get his hair cut anyway.' A fat boy holding a thin boy in a half-Nelson pushed his way past them.

'As a matter of fact,' Krippendorf said, 'I thought I would invite the parents in for drinks. There is no compelling reason why the young should have a monopoly on pleasure.'

'Ooh, lovely,' she said, bringing her hands together in a single clap. The top three buttons of her rugby jersey were undone and Krippendorf found himself gazing professionally into the dark cavity.

'I would of course run you back in the car. You know what the number fourteens are like.' He took out his wallet and handed her one of his printed address cards. She held it delicately between thumb and forefinger as though it were a photographic negative. 'It won't be a fancy do, will it?' A flicker of apprehension passed across her face.

'No, no, no, no, no. I envisage a thoroughly informal affair. Come just as you are.' He caught sight of Edmund emerging from the throng. He was trailing his new coat behind him by the sleeve, like an old man walking his dog.

Krippendorf said, 'Until Friday at six.' He bowed imperceptibly from the waist.

'See you.' She smiled congenially and trundled her buggy off towards a horde of children swarming up the railings.

Edmund's first words were, 'The school nurse came today. I've got nits.'

'Not again?'

'You've got to shampoo my hair with that chemical stuff and comb it with a metal comb.'

'I am perfectly familiar with the procedure by now.' He took his son's hand and led him in the direction of the corner sweetshop. It was already crowded with children poring over the sex magazines and stealing chocolate bars off the counter. 'I have been thinking,' Krippendorf said. 'It is time you had a party. You have not had a party since we celebrated the assassination of the Labour councillors.'

'My birthday isn't till August.' Edmund stood immobilized before the huge sweet counter.

'I was not thinking of your birthday.'

'What, then?'

'A party for the sheer fun of the thing. There is a case to be made for spontaneity.'

Edmund's hand moved indecisively above the chocolate wrappers. He picked up a bar of fruit and nut, put it down, then picked it up again. 'When could I have it?'

'Friday is the day I have in mind.'

'Saturday would be better. I go to the Jesuit disco on Fridays.'

'It will have to be on Friday.'

'But why?'

'The arrangements have now been made. Besides, there is no virtue in postponing pleasure. The Protestant ethic is an outworn doctrine.'

Edmund finally selected a chocolate marzipan bar coated with chopped brazil nuts and whipped orange caramel. Before his father had paid for it he had already torn off the wrapper and devoured half of it.

Outside the shop Krippendorf said, 'That nice little chap in your class, Leroy something-or-other . . . ?'

'Leroy Mendoza?'

'Yes.'

'He's a twit.'

Krippendorf cleared his throat. 'I think it would be a magnanimous gesture to invite him to your party.'

'Leroy Mendoza? Why?'

'He has a disadvantaged background. You must learn to be charitable to people less well off than yourself. The failure to do so only encourages Bolshevism.'

'But I can't stand him, he stinks.'

'Edmund,' he said sternly, 'there is no call to be racialist. I will not have it.'

'He's an Arsenal supporter. He's not coming.'

'Yes he is.'

Edmund pulled his father to a halt and looked up into his face. 'But he's not my friend.'

'Now is your opportunity to remedy the situation. We are no longer living in a monocultural society. Your friends and acquaintances should be drawn from a wider ethnic circle.'

Edmund wiped his sleeve across his mouth. 'Suppose I don't invite him?'

'No Leroy, no party.'

They walked past the bombed-out betting shop in silence, father and son hand in hand. A police car raced by, red light flashing, siren blaring. As they were stepping over the prostrate bodies of the meths drinkers Edmund said, 'How many friends could I invite?'

'Six, including Leroy.'

'Six plus Leroy,' countered Edmund.

'Done,' said his father.

He spent all Friday afternoon in the kitchen making jellies and blancmanges and cutting the crusts off slices of brown bread to make triangular sandwiches of chicken paste and chocolate spread. At six o'clock the house was full of children kicking the furniture and throwing water about. Krippendorf removed his apron when he spotted Leroy and his mother walking up the garden path.

'Sorry we're late,' Leroy's mother said. 'The buses are on a go-slow.'

'One can hardly tell the difference,' Krippendorf beamed as he carefully removed her coat.

'I would of got the tube but they're on strike.'

'I thought they were merely working to rule?'

'No, that was last week,' she said. 'It's the railways who are working to rule this week, same as the postmen.' She made Leroy wipe his perfectly dry shoes on the mat and tucked the back of his shirt inside his cords. He was clutching a badly wrapped packet which he handed to Edmund. 'Happy birthday,' he said.

'It's not my birthday.'

'Say thank you and open it,' his father instructed.

Edmund's curiosity got the better of his sullen resentment and he tore at the wrapping paper and Sellotape until he had revealed a cardboard box with a faded picture of Windsor Castle on the lid. When he shook it it rattled. 'A jigsaw puzzle,' he said. 'A bloody jigsaw puzzle.' He looked at his father in disbelief.

Krippendorf quickly took the box from him. 'Show Leroy downstairs to the games room.'

'We're in the middle of something.'

'Leroy can join in.'

'We've already got the right number.'

'Edmund.'

His son slouched off, followed reluctantly by Leroy. Moments later a series of loud crashes and screams of laughter and pain issued from the basement. Krippendorf smiled. 'It all sounds very Hobbesian,' he said. 'We had better leave them to it.' He took her into the living-room and opened the drinks cabinet. She gazed admiringly around the room, showing open curiosity about the framed pictures and damaged antiques.

'I thought all the parents were coming?' she said as he handed her a large gin and tonic.

'Alas, they were all otherwise engaged. I suspect they are all at home watching the televised hanging.'

After her second gin and tonic she became very talkative. After her third he was calling her Melba. Her father was a Filipino sailor who had jumped ship in Liverpool and later moved to London, where she herself was born and raised. She told him about her husband, a second-hand-furniture salesman who gambled and drank too much. 'He never used to beat me though. He was very good like that.' Her long braids were decorated with coloured wooden beads which she occasionally fingered as though telling the beads of a rosary. 'I was ever so glad when he left me,' she said. 'He ran off with this bird he met in the hair transplant clinic. Skinny little cow she was too.' She went on to tell him about her younger brother's impending trial on a breaking-and-entering charge, and about the recent episode on the Bakerloo line when she was molested by an elderly woman in a kilt. Krippendorf half-listened to what she was saying, sometimes murmuring in agreement or tut-tutting in appropriate places. He shifted about in his chair, observing her photogenic properties and visualizing the effects he might get with the sensitive use of backlighting.

'Anyway,' she was saying, 'I told them to mind their own bleeding business. I said if I want to invite a bloke back for the night that's down to me I said. They hide in the street with binoculars and notebooks and then try to stop my payments.' There was a muffled bang in the basement and then the sound of glass being shattered. She stopped in mid-sentence and gave him an enquiring glance.

'The party is warming up,' he said. He collected her empty glass and filled it to the top with equal proportions of gin and tonic. She recounted the fine details of the blazing row she had had that very morning with the checkout girl in Sainsbury's over an expired gift coupon, and told him about the time she had waited all day in the rain to wave to the Queen Mother. At seven-thirty she said she ought to go.

'Time for just one more, Melba, surely?'

'Just a quick one then.' She was lounging back in the deep sofa, no longer bothering to prevent her short polyester skirt from riding up around her thighs. She had slender thighs and curiously shiny calves. One of her shoes had fallen off. It lay upturned on the carpet like something left over from a disaster. Twenty minutes later when she rose to go she wobbled uncertainly and Krippendorf held out a solicitous hand to steady her. His face brushed against her braids as he did so, causing her beads to rattle. Be careful, he thought.

They found Leroy alone in the basement. He was tied to a chair with strips of material that Krippendorf recognized as having been his flowery Jaeger shirt. 'I'm Great Eagle,' he said. 'I've been captured by the enemy, but my braves will be coming to rescue me soon.'

Krippendorf cut him free and filled his pockets with sweets. He fetched a large plastic carrier-bag and filled it with as many of Edmund's toys as it would hold. 'Edmund wanted you to have these,' he said.

He helped Melba on with her coat and led them to the car. 'I don't know about the kids,' she said, laughing throatily, 'but I've had a smashing time.' She was still unsteady on her feet and he held her arm as he guided her path through the overflowing garbage bags and the dogshit.

Leroy sat in the back seat of the car playing with his new toys. He pointed his space gun at elderly pedestrians and made explosive noises with his lips. Krippendorf drove at a leisurely pace through the light evening traffic, following

Melba's directions. She sometimes said left when she meant right, but not consistently enough for him to reverse the meaning of her words. He took it as a favourable omen when she switched on the car radio without asking and began humming the words of the egregious melody. Presently they came to a block of high-rise council flats and he pulled up alongside a leafless tree with a supermarket trolley lodged among the boughs.

'Home sweet home,' Melba sighed. 'Out you get, Leroy. And what do you say?'

'Thank you for having me,' Leroy said mechanically.

Melba laughed her throaty laugh. 'You'll be too old to say that soon.' She turned to Krippendorf, making no move to get out. 'You want to come in? I only got tea and stuff.' She lowered her false eyelashes.

'I really ought to be getting back.'

'Yeah.'

'I have to shave Edmund's head again.'

He allowed a small silence to develop. Melba's hand was resting on her bare knee, one inch from his own. He felt certain he could have touched it, a small innocent gesture presaging so much. He cleared his throat. 'Melba?'

'Mm?'

'Concerning the invitation to tea. Were you to invite me for tomorrow I should accept with alacrity.'

She looked directly at him, half-smiling, her lips pursed, as though carefully weighing all the implications. 'Okay,' she said huskily. 'I hope I can find me best tablecloth.'

On Monday afternoon he took her to see a movie about a pretty girl dying of an incurable disease in picturesque surroundings. She cried copiously at the unhappy ending and all through the following short about the migration patterns of Canada geese. He put a consoling arm around her and gave her his monogrammed handkerchief to blow into.

The following day they had lunch together in the snug bar of the Carpenters' Arms. Melba was wearing a thin cheesecloth shirt that seemed several sizes too small. All through his scampi-in-a-basket he had the uneasy feeling that at any moment her powerful breasts would burst out of their confinement. He stared in fascination at the flimsy material and inadequate buttons as they held fast against the strain.

'I can see you're a tits man,' she said, laughing into her pint of stout.

'I beg your pardon?'

'You never take your eyes off them.'

As they were leaving the pub she slipped her arm inside his. Although there was no one else in the street, he moved her braids to one side and whispered something in her ear. 'Naughty boy,' she said.

That same evening he made a pot of black coffee and took it to his study. Dispensing with his usual ritual preliminaries he began at once to write. The words poured fluently from his pen as though they had been stored inside it waiting for release.

Shelmikedmu are obsessed by the fear of witchcraft. Men and women alike believe that almost all young females in the society are actual or potential witches who are capable of causing calamity and misfortune to strike as the whim takes them. The source of a witch's power is a substance that is manufactured and stored in the female breast. Shelmikedmu believe that the bigger a woman's breasts the greater her powers of black magic. Well-endowed girls are very conscious of their latent powers. They are often to be seen strutting and posturing around the village, provoking looks of awe and wonderment on the faces of the men. Only males can be bewitched, and a man always shows such women great respect, ever fearful of having a malevolent nipple pointed in his direction.

Young women with a visibly large supply of witchcraft substance (*monxqlu*) are greatly prized as wives. This is because a woman cannot bewitch her own husband, and also because the only antidote against one woman's witchcraft is another woman's counter-witchcraft. A man will often turn his wife's powers to personal advantage by getting her to direct a nipple at his enemies. Consequently, men are careful to avoid picking quarrels with other men whose wives are more dangerously equipped than their own.

A man married to a woman with plenteous witchcraft substance usually enjoys a deep sense of supernatural security. His peace of mind, however, gradually evaporates as his wife ages. He then inspects her anxiously each morning for signs of detumescence and decay. Some believe that the storehouse of witchcraft substance can be preserved in its prime condition if it is properly treated and maintained. It is a very common sight to see men massaging their wives with iguana fat in an attempt to delay shrinkage. The Dutch missionary who ministered to the village often volunteered to undertake this chore as a pastoral service to his younger converts. He claimed that this practice, and the general belief in witchcraft substance, was not in the least at variance with the more enlightened teachings of the modern church . . .

In the Shelmikedmu language a highly refined terminology has evolved to classify and identify the many different species and varieties of witchcraft substance. Thus, there are seventeen terms to describe different types of nipple, and twenty-two terms for our single word 'cleavage'. A man can always recognize and name at a glance any of the principal species of bosom. (See

Appendix IV for a full glossary of terms and illustrations.)

Krippendorf was trying to mend a hole in Mickey's grey school trousers. The only cotton he could find was pink. He sewed the hole up with large looping stitches, only to discover that he had sewn both legs together. He ripped out the cotton, pinched the jagged edges of the hole together to form a large lip, and stapled it down with a stapling machine. He was about to employ the same technique on a torn pyjama jacket when Edmund's discordant wail cut through the always precarious silence.

He went upstairs to investigate and found Edmund kneeling at the side of his hamster's cage. 'Ms Molly's dead,' he whimpered, pointing to the inert and shapeless bundle of matted fur that was only just distinguishable from the bed of wood shavings and ruined socks on which it lay.

Krippendorf opened the window before taking his son in his arms. 'How long has she been dead?' he asked, breathing in as little air as possible.

'I don't know.'

'When did you last feed her?'

'I thought you were feeding her,' Edmund sobbed.

Krippendorf dried his son's face, dabbing at the familiar amalgam of tears and snot with the corner of the Paddington Bear duvet cover. 'Never mind,' he said. 'I shall take you to the pet shop tomorrow and get another one. Though perhaps a goldfish would be preferable.'

Edmund's thin body convulsed in a fresh wave of sobbing. 'I don't want another one. I only want Ms Molly. I love Ms Molly.'

Krippendorf rocked his son in his arms like a baby. He could not imagine the death of any human, including himself, provoking such inconsolable grief. The noise attracted Mickey, who clumped into the room on his new roller skates.

'He did it,' cried Edmund, pointing a wet finger at his brother.

'No I didn't,' retorted Mickey at once. 'Did what, anyway?'

'He was always doing things to Ms Molly,' Edmund snivelled. 'He used her for his chemical warfare game.'

'Mickey, I have asked you not to play that game,' said his father sternly. 'It is causing the paint to peel off the landing walls.'

Mickey bent down to inspect the body in the cage. 'We ought to bury it in the garden,' he said. 'We could make a proper grave for it.'

Edmund suddenly perked up. 'With a wooden cross and a nice tombstone,' he croaked.

'We could have a real burial service,' Mickey added.

'Yes, with hymns and prayers, like we did for Nana.' Edmund freed himself from his father's embrace. 'We can dress up in robes and things. We can't wear ordinary clothes.' His face was now alight with anticipated pleasure as he began rummaging through his chest of drawers in search of clothing that could be adapted to ceremonial use. 'I need something red for a cloak,' he said. 'I know . . .' He went running out of the room and a few moments later Krippendorf heard the ominous sound of fabric being ripped.

Twenty minutes later he found them in the garden digging a hole with the coal shovel. They had made a cross out of the bamboo stick he had been using to support a young clematis. Edmund began lining the hole with pages torn from the current telephone directory while Mickey carved the initials R.I.P. in the breadboard.

'What are you using for the coffin?' Krippendorf enquired. 'I seem to recognize it.'

'It's Shelley's trinket box,' Mickey explained. 'It looks better painted black.'

The two boys dressed themselves in their home-made robes while discussing the arrangements for the burial service. 'Dad, you can say something in Latin,' Edmund proposed. He pushed his arms through the newly-made holes in the living-room curtain. 'And Mickey, you'll have to take your roller skates off. Everything's got to be done properly.' He looked immensely happy as he fussed about with the tea-cosy on his head and fashioned a wreath from peonies and dandelions. When everything was prepared to his satisfaction Mickey was sent in to carry down the corpse of Ms Molly.

'Is anything wrong, Mr K.?' Mrs O'Shea's face materialized above the fence, ready to be shocked.

'I am afraid so. There has been an unfortunate death in the family.'

'Oh dear,' she said, clapping a hand against her loose-skinned throat.

'It was wholly unexpected. Everyone is quite distraught.'

Her small eyes glinted. 'It's not Mickey, is it?'

'I am afraid not, Mrs O'Shea. Mickey is his usual robust self.'

As though to corroborate this verdict on his health Mickey's excited shouts rang out from inside the house. He came stumbling out, still on roller skates. 'Look,' he cried, 'Ms Molly's recovered.' The hamster was wriggling energetically in his arms. He set it down on the grass and it took a few tentative steps forward before stopping to nibble at the dock leaves and the bindweed.

Edmund made no move. His face was like an unexploded bomb. 'The fucking thing,' he screamed. 'After all the trouble we've gone through. Now everything's ruined.'

The hamster was turning around and around in ever diminishing circles and pointlessly twitching its nose. Krippendorf watched in astonishment as Edmund gathered up his robes, shuffled quickly forward, and struck the hamster three fierce blows on the head with the coal shovel. It lay on its side, completely still. Next to it lay the tea-cosy that had fallen off as a result of Edmund's exertions. He bent over the limp body and turned it over with his foot. 'She's really dead this time,' he announced. 'Now we can have the funeral.'

Melba hesitated in the doorway, surveying the scene carefully before entering. 'Posh bedroom,' she said. She walked about the room admiring the custom-made curtains and the beechwood wardrobe, picking things up and putting them down in exactly the same place. She had taken off her shoes at the door and was holding them by the straps. She stepped carefully on tiptoe like a child in a forbidden place. 'You sure it's all right?' she whispered. 'Your wife and that?'

'She is in Tripoli, I believe, filming the assassination squads.' He closed the bedroom door but did not turn the key in the lock. Earlier he had changed the sheets on the bed and put Veronica's jewellery out of sight.

Melba skipped over to him on her toes and placed both arms around his neck, still holding her shoes by the straps. He had to dip his body to make this possible. The first time they had kissed had been in the back seat of a number fourteen bus during the go-slow. The second time had been in the snug bar of the Carpenters' Arms next to an old man with catarrh. This time she closed her eyes and forced her tongue between his teeth. He could feel it wriggling about in his mouth like a small captive animal.

'I got to go at three,' she said. 'I'm taking Leroy to the psychiatrist about his dreams.' She let the hand holding her shoes rest on his shoulder while using the other to unfasten the buttons of her blouse.

'I suppose you want to take my bra off?' she enquired. 'I know blokes like to do that.'

Krippendorf reached behind her and fiddled with the hook and eye until the lace-edged brassiere suddenly fell away. Her witchcraft substance seemed to cascade out. He stepped back involuntarily, as though instinctively aware of the danger he might be in. Her nipples were pointing directly at him in the militant position. He felt his blood draining away.

'It's all right,' Melba assured him. 'They won't bite you.' She took his hands and placed them on her breasts. 'Nice?'

Krippendorf handled them with great delicacy, conscious of their extraordinary powers. 'They are remarkable,' he confessed. 'In some languages there is a special term for them.'

'Tits?'

'For this particular genus. Our own classificatory vocabulary is so impoverished by comparison.'

Melba hooked her thumbs inside the waistband of her skirt and pulled it down together with her knickers in a single economical movement.

'On reflection,' he said, 'that is something of a paradox.'

'You what?' She was folding her clothes in an orderly pile on Veronica's dressing-table.

He pressed his fingertips together meditatively. 'Given the tremendous interest in that part of the body, in western culture at least, one might have supposed that an adequate descriptive nomenclature would by now have evolved. Just ponder a moment. Does it not strike you as anomalous that anatomical objects which are so palpably venerated, and so proudly displayed, should nevertheless fail to yield a set of classificatory terms designed to capture their multiple forms and varieties?' He tapped his pockets in search of something to write with. His best ideas often seemed to come at inconvenient times. 'After all, the Eskimos have a dozen or more names for different types of snow . . .'

'Look, are you coming to bed or not?' Melba said. Before getting under the covers herself she had drawn the curtains, declaring it to be unnatural to lie in bed in the full light of day.

He undressed and climbed in beside her while still mulling over the classification problem. She began telling him about her fight with a neighbour over a disputed dustbin and the devastation caused to Leroy's socks by his sweating feet. After a while, Krippendorf slid furtively down beneath the covers and rested his head on her small round stomach. He gently eased her legs apart and put his face between her thighs. He could now only just hear her talking about the time she went on a day trip to Milton Keynes and almost turned religious. Her bush felt prickly against his lips as his tongue explored the moist and convoluted folds beneath.

'Hey,' she called out, as if suddenly aware of his absence. 'What you up to down there?' She flung aside the covers, revealing his unauthorized activity. 'Don't be so mucky.'

Krippendorf peered up at her from the darkness between her thighs. His lips were glistening and she handed him a tissue from the man-size Kleenex box. 'Wipe your mouth,' she said. 'You're not kissing me like that.'

He lay beside her on his back and looked at the shadows flickering on the ceiling. The whole thing was proving even more burdensome than he had expected. Soon she began to talk about the bigoted shop steward in the cat-meat factory where she used to work before the redundancies. He slid his arm beneath the small of her back and rolled her across on top of him.

'Now what you doing?' She raised the top half of her body, hands flat on either side of him, like someone doing press-ups. Her witchcraft substance swung menacingly against his face. 'You're the man,' she explained. 'You're supposed to be the one on top.'

She patiently rearranged their bodies to her liking. 'There, isn't that better?' She folded her legs around him.

'It does make a change.'

Melba laughed her throaty laugh. 'You got some funny ideas for an educated man.' Presently she fell silent and closed her eyes. Krippendorf began to do what convention, circumstance and his higher purpose all required him to do. After what seemed a very short time she gave a quiet whimper, arched her back, and then lay absolutely still. He felt strangely alone, stranded on her body, having no further function.

'Sorry I come so quick,' she said, opening her eyes. 'I'm always like that. I keep meaning to go to the doctor about it.'

'It is quite all right.' He started to disengage.

'Did you come?' she asked.

'Yes.'

'No you didn't, I can feel you didn't.' She wiggled her hips in confirmation.

'It really does not matter.'

'No, I want you to.'

'I am perfectly satisfied.'

'You can't be, it's not natural. You got to have a proper come. I'll be really choked if you don't.'

He sighed heavily. 'Very well then.' She lay motionless beneath him as his long body rose and fell upon her. His dandruff powdered her dark skin. He was acutely aware of the way she was watching him all the while in open fascination. When he fell for the last time she kissed him on the shoulder and said in a sprightly voice, 'There, you liked that, didn't you? I knew you would.'

'It was most agreeable.'

She wrapped his maggot in paper tissues like a soft expensive fruit. He lit a cigarette and they puffed at it in turns while she tried to recall the words of the new smash-hit single about pacifists in love. Shortly after three-fifteen she jumped out of bed and started hurriedly to dress. Krippendorf propped himself up on the pillow and observed her movements with studied interest as she bent and turned in front of the long oval mirror.

'Melba?' he said nonchalantly.

'Mm?'

'Do you like having your picture taken?'

'Course I do.' She was straining to fasten her bra-strap at the back, screwing her eyes shut in concentration.

'I have recently bought a decent foreign camera and some photographic equipment, also foreign.'

'Me left side's me best,' she said. 'I got a small scar on the right where Leroy threw his home computer at me.'

'I shall bear that in mind.'

She pulled on her skirt and tucked in her blouse. She had to breathe in hard to fasten the waistband of her very tight skirt. 'Are you any good at it?' She let out a spluttering laugh. 'At photography I mean.'

Krippendorf reached for another tissue. 'I am learning all the time. Tomorrow when you come I shall show you exactly what I have learned so far.'

Four

It had started one or two days before as a slight discomfort but was now quite definitely the onset of a pain. He shifted experimentally in his seat and eased the crutch of his trousers with one hand as he turned the pages of *Flora and Fauna of Amazonia* with the other. It was still raining outside and the reference library was fuller than usual of crumpled men sleeping noisily over the trade journals. In the next seat a man in a steaming overcoat was feeding himself with small pieces of bread which he kept concealed beneath a cunningly constructed pile of foreign dictionaries. Krippendorf had lost count of the number of times he had politely declined the man's gestural invitation to help himself.

The twinges of pain grew more frequent and intense. Presently he left the library and walked through the rain to the public lavatory opposite the street market. Men in damp coats were standing shoulder to shoulder facing the white porcelain, legs astride, heads lowered, never glancing to one side. Behind each man stood another awaiting his turn. Krippendorf joined the third cohort that was just beginning to form, his shoes squelching on the soft carpet of rotten fruit and sodden lavatory paper. Two of the three WCs had signs on the door saying 'Out of Order'. From the interior of the third there rang out a cacophony of trumpeting, splashing and grunting sounds, as of elephants or wild pigs running through marshland in a state of panic.

Krippendorf stepped up to take his place at the urinal,

deftly shielding his maggot from the public gaze with a cupped hand. A searing sensation accompanied each jet that he aimed at the manufacturer's name on the porcelain. Specks of yellow-white discharge were visible on his athletic underpants. He felt inhibited in his inspection by the apparent interest of the man to his left and the intimations of urgency from the man immediately behind who was now running quickly on the spot.

He washed his hands under the cold tap of the blocked-up hand basin. The warm air blower remained inert when he pushed the red button and the towel from the machine was trailing along the floor, grey, wet and desolate.

He crossed the road and stood in line for the one telephone kiosk in the row of six that was still functioning. Twenty minutes later he was dialling the number he had memorized from the poster in the lavatory.

'STD clinic,' said a girl's voice.

'I should like to speak to the doctor.'

'Do you wish to make an appointment, sir?'

Krippendorf stared back at his wracked face in the small square mirror. 'I suppose so.'

'Wednesday the tenth at two-fifteen?'

'Nothing before then?'

'I'm afraid not, sir. There's a very big demand at this time of year.'

The clinic was a prefabricated hut behind the car park of the main hospital. The chairs were hard and upright and there were no colourful magazines on the grey metal table. Six other people were before him. They sat still and silent, avoiding each other's eyes like people travelling in a lift. Shortly after three-thirty he was called for his two-fifteen appointment.

The sign on the door said Dr J. H. R. Kesby. Krippendorf knocked and went straight in. A burly figure in a white coat sat at a desk making notes with a silly pen. He looked up and squinted at Krippendorf through pebble lens glasses. 'Good Lord.' he said. 'It *is* you. I thought there couldn't be many with your name.' He pressed himself back in his swivel chair.

Krippendorf stared at him uncomprehendingly. 'I beg your pardon?'

'Toytown,' the doctor said. 'You were at Toytown. We were there at the same time.'

It was many years since Krippendorf had heard this disrespectful sobriquet for his former university.

'I used to run the Medical Centre. I had a beard in those days, like everyone else.' He ran a hand over his smooth blue jowls.

Krippendorf nodded in half-recognition. He had a vague recollection of someone with a reputation for making pretty girls undress when they went to him with migraine.

'You left shortly before me, as I recall,' the doctor continued. 'Wasn't there a spot of bother in your department? At the time of the redundancies?' He took off his glasses and pressed his eyes with thumb and middle finger, trying to get the past into sharper focus. 'Now what the hell was it all about?'

Krippendorf cleared his throat and said, 'There was a feud between the neo-structuralists and the symbolic inter-actionists. The symbolic interactionists won.'

'Aha,' the doctor said. He seemed about to make a note of it. 'And what have you been up to since?'

Krippendorf heaved his broad shoulders. 'This and that. A spot of fieldwork, the occasional publication. As a matter of fact I have another piece coming out this week.'

'Freelance stuff?'

'In a manner of speaking.'

The doctor reminisced for a while about old times and people they knew in common, like the Professor of Greek who had since become a male stripper, and the Senior Lecturer in Econometrics who had used his redundancy pay to open a vegetarian restaurant on a barge.

Then, a different tone of voice, he said, 'So. And what brings you here?'

Krippendorf did not feel in a sufficiently jocular mood to say his tonsils or his carburettor. Instead, he dropped his trousers to his knees and pointed to his infirm maggot.

The doctor looked at it as though it was the first time he had seen one. He covered his hand with a thin plastic bag and began jabbing and pushing at Krippendorf's delicate parts. 'Yes,' he said, 'it looks like a straightforward dose of clap. I'll have to take a swab and send it to the lab. In the meantime I'll give you a shot of penicillin.' He busied himself with swabs and needles, humming as he did so the words of a once popular song.

'You've had it before, I suppose?' he said matter-of-factly.

Krippendorf shook his head.

'Really? I'm surprised you managed to avoid it in Toytown. It became an epidemic.'

'So I believe. I once had to cancel a lecture on polyandry because of the lack of an audience.' He winced as the endlessly long needle went in.

The doctor laughed. 'It was commonly known as mousy tongue.'

'Mousy tongue?'

'After the Chinese leader. The revolutionary students used to get their girl friends to infect the professors in a bid to destroy the system from within.'

Krippendorf hitched up his trousers and zipped up his fly with great care. After the injection he was in twice as much pain as before.

'You probably know the drill,' the doctor said. 'No alcohol, and no sex for at least three weeks.' He said this with a certain amount of relish. 'By the way, do you know the . . . ah . . . source of the infection?'

'I have a pretty good idea.'

'You'd better get in touch with her right away. She'll

need treatment too.' He was holding his hands under running water. 'It is a she, I suppose?'

'It is.'

The doctor dried his hands on a paper towel and began scribbling something incomprehensible on a prescription pad with his silly pen. 'You're a married man, aren't you?'

'I am.'

'Have you told your wife?'

'Not yet.'

The doctor leaned forward confidentially. 'I'll give you the same advice I give to all married men. Come clean, ha, ha.'

Krippendorf smiled dutifully at the feeble joke.

'Seriously, though, you'd be well advised to tell the lady-wife all. She'll find out anyway when she sees the stains on the bedsheets and the state of your underpants. I don't know what kind of woman your wife is, but I dare say she'd rather know the truth than wake up one morning and find herself pissing razorblades.'

A Note on Shelmikedmu Conceptions of Disease

Shelmikedmu believe that all diseases are punishments for bad behaviour. Sickness of any kind is therefore regarded as evidence of unShelmikedmu conduct.

A person who falls ill is immediately put on trial in order that the nature of his crime may be established. Since guilt has already been proven, by virtue of the punishment inflicted, the medico-judicial process is concerned with discovering what the condemned are actually guilty of.

Sick people are often surprised to learn of their own wickedness, and occasionally they question the findings of the court. The trial of an elderly widow, who had lost almost all her protective witchcraft substance, dragged on for more than a week before she finally confessed that her rheumatoid arthritis was due to her complicity in the failure of the mango crop. Those who enjoy good health are, by this very token, law-abiding citizens. Shelmikedmu know that a person could not act untribally without being brought down by sickness. Thus, if a man makes off with his neighbour's wife or his best broom and does not become ill immediately after, he cannot be considered guilty of any offence. He is regarded as having been the rightful owner of these things in the first place, even though to all outward appearances they belonged to somebody else.

When my houseboy fell sick with rabies he was found guilty of conducting an illicit affair with the village headman's favourite wife, even though it was widely known that the person she was consorting with at night was the robust and healthy Dutch missionary.

Krippendorf sat propped up in bed against two plump pillows trying to read an espionage thriller. After every couple of pages he had to turn back, unable to fathom what had happened to whom and why. It seemed that a body had been discovered between the goalposts in Wembley Stadium during the Cup Final. While preparing to face a penalty kick the goalkeeper had complained to the referee of unevenness in the ground. Earlier, a nun had been kidnapped in the Dordogne by a man with an artificial leg, and later there occurred an apparently crucial but enigmatic encounter between a jam tycoon and a balloon seller in some unspecified oriental city.

The book slipped from his hands for the third time just as the front door slammed. He readjusted the pillows, switched off the bedside lamp and pulled the duvet up to his chin. Veronica swept into the bedroom and turned on the light. 'Jamie,' she cooed in a childlike voice.

He made no response other than to increase the guttural quality of his breathing.

'Stop pretending,' she said. 'I know you're awake, I saw your light on from outside.'

Without opening his eyes he said sleepily, 'Are you drunk again?'

'I might be, I'm not really sure. My driving was absolutely faultless.'

'That is how it would seem if you were drunk.'

She laughed merrily and allowed herself to fall full length on top of him. 'Shut up and give us a kiss.' She ruffled his hair, untroubled by the fact that it was not really thick enough to accommodate this gesture.

'Is it a good idea to wear your boots and all your clothes in bed?' he asked as she climbed beneath the covers.

'Yes it is,' she said. 'I'm in the mood to be poked with all my clothes on.' She forced her tongue into his mouth as far as it would go.

When he was next able to speak he said, 'Actually, I have a bit of a head.' He made a face like someone with a headache in an aspirin advertisement. 'I think it may be this novel I am reading.'

'Balls. 'That was your excuse last night. The night before it was your back.'

'I had been overdoing it at the ironing-board. It is a little too low for me.'

Veronica propped herself up on one elbow and said solemnly, 'Jamie, do you realize you've only poked me once since I got back from Caracas?'

'Are you quite sure?'

'Positive.' She fumbled in her overcoat pocket and took out a diary. 'The last time was on the ninth, the same day as the Accrington riots. And even then you made us hurry so that you wouldn't miss the Buster Keaton movie.'

'It is rarely shown on television.'

She threw her diary to one side and clambered roughly across him, pulling up her long suede skirt and placing her knees either side of him. Krippendorf's hand was inside his pyjama trousers endeavouring to remove the wad of cotton wool that encased the head of his suppurating maggot. Feigning an attack of cramp, he managed to dislodge the cotton wool and push it down the leg of his pyjama trousers.

'Anyway,' Veronica said, giving a disorderly laugh, 'I want my conjugal rights and I want them *now*. She plunged her head forward and enclosed her lips around his flaccid maggot. Grasping it at the root she began sucking noisily on the tip in a manner that reminded him of Edmund's handling of an ice-lolly. He could feel it enlarging against his will as he struggled to conjure up counter-erotic thoughts. He mumbled the words of his school boating song; he conjugated irregular Greek verbs; he thought of the smell and texture of Mickey's socks; he rehearsed the complexities of Shelmikedmu suicide rules. None of his efforts could neutralize the effect of Veronica's mobile lips and lubricious tongue.

Finally she raised her head and pointed in triumph at his treacherously upright maggot. 'Yummy, yummy,' she cried. After some painful manhandling she managed to steer it inside the leg of her knickers.

'Veronica,' he said, 'there is a matter we ought to discuss.'

'Be quiet. Just lie back and enjoy it.' She wriggled about on him as though trying to get comfortable on an unfamiliar chair. Before long her movements became more rhythmical and her face changed colour and shape. Then followed the breathless snorts and the Joycean babble.

'Christ, I needed that,' she gasped as she rolled off him and fell asleep in her clothes.

Krippendorf scooped up the morning mail and took it into the kitchen. The children were milling about in various states of undress and complaining about the absence of their favourite cereals. The sugar bowl was empty and he had to scavenge about among the milk puddles and the crusts of incinerated toast beneath the table and chairs for the one spoonful needed to make his instant coffee palatable.

'I can only find one brown shoe,' Mickey whined. He was trying to knot his tie with one hand while spooning up Rice Krispies with the other.

'You were certainly wearing two yesterday,' his father said. 'One on each foot.'

'I think I lost one on the bus during the fight.'

'In which case you will have to hop to school. Fortunately it is not too slippery.'

'Is my Superman vest dry yet?' Edmund stood shivering in his Superman underpants, his thin arms wrapped around his thin chest.

'It is still in the oven,' Krippendorf said. 'Give it another two minutes.'

'Last time you said that it melted,' Edmund reminded him. 'My favourite vest, too.'

'Man-made fibres are unpredictable.' He buttered a slice of cold toast, prodding gingerly with his knife at the butter dish to avoid the deposits of plum jam and Marmite. 'What are you doing with your mother's clothes?' he asked Shelley. She was folding skirts and dresses into neat piles and transferring them to a canvas holdall.

'It's for the refugees. We're collecting things at school. I showed you the note.'

He fingered one of Veronica's ankle-length Liberty-print skirts. 'But these are all new.'

'Well of course they are. You don't think I would give them any old junk, do you?'

'Have you asked your mother?'

'She's still asleep. You know she gets grumpy if we wake her.'

He felt something wet on the seat of his pyjamas and rose to find he had been sitting on the remains of Edmund's porridge. 'She may not be terribly pleased,' he said, dabbing at himself with a tea-cloth.

'Why not?' Shelley said in surprise. 'She's always saying the rich should help the poor.'

'Shelley, you must try and grasp the difference between theory and practice.'

She zipped up the holdall and struggled with it to the door. 'I'll collect some of your things tomorrow,' she warned.

When the last of the children had left for school he cleared away the breakfast debris and sorted through the mail. There were three letters addressed to him. One of them was printed in several colours with seals and tabs attached. It advised him that he might qualify for a free holiday for two in Tenerife if he could correctly identify the six pairs of famous eyes on the enclosed form and compose a limerick extolling the virtues of underfloor heating to be judged by a panel of experts whose decision was absolutely final. The second letter was an invitation to join the Dog Lovers' Book Club, which he immediately tore in shreds. The third letter was from the editor of *Exotica*.

Dear Krippendorf,

Please find enclosed our cheque for £750 in payment for your illustrated article entitled 'Witchcraft and Wittgenstein: Utterances as a Mode of Social Control'. A revised and abbreviated version of this article was published in our last issue under the title 'Amazonian Knockers'.

All of us here were delighted with your photographs – she really is a most eye-catching and impressive informant. It took us some time to decide which of your compositions to use for our centrefold feature. Personally, I favoured the self-mortification study, but my Art Editor persuaded me of the aesthetic virtues of the spirit-frenzy pose. Readership response has fully justified my faith in his judgement; we have been inundated with orders for our poster-size enlargement.

We have also received a large number of requests for more illustrated articles on your tribe. They really do seem to have captured the anthropological imagination. Our plans are now well advanced for the introduction of a monthly pull-out supplement on the general theme of 'Savage Maidenhood'. We should be extremely pleased to receive more examples of your scholarship to include in this venture. Do you have anything in your files that would be suitable to get the project off to a flying start? I look forward to hearing from you.

> Yours sincerely,
> Alastair Dunkerley,
> Managing Editor,
> Exotica Enterprises and Anthropological
> Tours Ltd.

Krippendorf was slumped in front of the television set watching a man with a bad haircut explaining science. Whilst staring fixedly at the teleprompter the man succeeded in rolling coloured ping-pong balls down a plastic tube and into a row of empty goldfish bowls. As he did so, he smiled occasionally to show that the laws of physics could be fun. On the new educational channel they were showing another documentary play about unemployed teenagers in the north arguing inarticulately in shop doorways. He switched to BBC 2 in time to see a simpering woman standing in front of a map of the British Isles and pinning

paper rainclouds over almost all of it. She smiled apologeti-
cally, as though she might be held personally responsible.

The front door slammed and Veronica came in holding a
Harrods' shopping bag in one hand and an executive
briefcase in the other. She immediately poured herself a
malt whisky and took a couple of deep gulps. 'Do you mind
if I turn that thing off?' she said. 'There's something I want
to say to you.' Without waiting for his reply she flicked the
switch and sat cross-legged on the floor. She picked at a
loose strand on her skirt and announced, 'It seems I've got
the pox.'

Krippendorf straightened himself in his chair. Beneath
the immediate sense of alarm was a curious feeling of relief
that the moment had finally come.

'I went to see the quack a couple of days ago,' she said.
'He confirmed it today.'

Krippendorf ran his hand back and forth along the arm of
the sofa, raising the pile and smoothing it flat again. 'Might
he not have made a mistake? Your chap usually has. He is
always diagnosing legionnaire's disease.'

Veronica shook her head in the decisive manner she had.
'No, I was pretty sure it was the clap before I went to him. I
recognized the symptoms.'

'They are very recognizable.'

She lit a cigarette with the stub of the one she had just
finished and blew smoke in the direction of the Hockney
reproduction. 'It's completely inexcusable,' she said. 'And
so humiliating.' She looked at him with an expression he
took to be profound contempt, though it might have been
ordinary hatred.

'I know how you must feel . . .' he began.

'Apologies don't really help.'

'I suppose not.' His carefully rehearsed phrases were
colliding in his head. He got up and poured himself a
drink.

'But I do apologize,' she said. 'I really am *very* sorry.'

84

broken glass. When he looked up from below the hand was still there.

He found Melba's flat at the third attempt.

'What you want?' she snapped angrily. She seemed about to slam the door in his face.

'I need to speak to you. It is quite important.'

Melba's eyes were full of mistrust. 'I'm not coming round your place again, if that's what you want. Not after that last time.'

Krippendorf raised his hands in a gesture of reassurance. 'No, no. This is nothing to do with photography. I promise you.'

She put her head out and scanned the balcony as though looking for evidence for the real purpose of his visit. A woman in a yashmak went by carrying a string bag full of lemonade bottles. 'What is it you want, then?'

'It is rather personal. Might I come in?'

After some hesitation she stood aside to let him pass. 'Don't you go trying no funny business neither,' she warned. He went through to the small sitting-room that was made even smaller by the dralon three-piece suite and mahogany-veneer sideboard. He occupied the narrow oblong of space in the centre of the room and stood very still. On his previous visit he had kept knocking over her plaster ornaments. He now adopted a slightly stooping posture, hands clasped behind his back, in the manner of royalty being called upon to inspect technology.

'I am here on the doctor's advice,' he said.

'What doctor?' She looked at him disbelievingly.

'The maggot doctor.'

'You trying to be funny?'

'The venereal specialist. The fact of the matter is, I have contracted gonorrhoea.'

'You what?' Melba sat down heavily in one of the dralon armchairs.

'I believe it is known in the vernacular as the clap.'

'I know what it bloody is,' she said, pressing her head back on the antimacassar. From a room above or from next door came the sound of bronchial coughing.

'You will need to seek treatment,' Krippendorf said. 'Penicillin will normally suffice, though in acute cases this may have to be supplemented by . . .'

'What you're telling me,' she said, 'is that you've landed me with a dose. That's bloody marvellous that is, that's really nice. That's all I sodding needed.' Her hand moved swiftly across to a plaster statuette of a whistling urchin. She lifted it up, straightened the polyester doily on which it stood, and put it down again.

Krippendorf cleared his throat. 'There appears to be some misunderstanding. 'I did not transmit the infection to you. It is I who am the recipient and you who are the donor, so to speak.'

Melba jumped out of the chair, her wooden hair beads clattering wildly about her face. 'Fucking cheek!' she shouted. 'Trying to land the blame on me. I reckon you got a fucking nerve coming here and accusing me.'

He stared at the tiny patch of patterned carpet visible on either side of his feet. It was proving much more difficult than he had anticipated. 'No particular blame attaches,' he said benignly. 'In this enlightened age the question of culpability is hardly . . .'

'Piss off!' Melba screamed. 'Fuck off out of here!' She pushed him towards the door with the flat of her hands. Furniture was being shifted about carelessly in the room immediately above. It seemed to Krippendorf extremely close to his head. Something had begun to worry him. 'Melba, are you absolutely sure?' he said. 'I can describe the symptoms to you.'

'Out. There's nothing wrong with my symptoms.' She pushed at him again.

He felt a sudden need to sit down somewhere quiet and work things out. Veronica's confession was nagging at the back of his mind. Could it really have come from her after all? His lips puckered with distaste at the thought of the chubby little man with badges on his lapel. 'Do you have a calendar I might borrow?' he asked. 'And a sheet of rough paper?'

Melba was pulling hard with both hands at the sleeve of his jacket.

'I may have made a bad mistake,' he said. 'I think I owe you an apology. The aetiology of sexually transmitted diseases is a complicated matter. You could hardly call it an exact science.'

Still gripping his sleeve, Melba kicked him forcefully on the shin with her stockinged foot. She winced with pain and tried to bite his arm through the thick Harris tweed.

Heavy footsteps sounded on the stairs and then a sandy-haired man appeared, buttoning up his shirt and coughing. His unshaven face was creased with the lines of interrupted sleep. 'What's all the racket about?' he asked. He had a Scottish inner-city accent that Krippendorf associated with bottle fights and people being sick on the pavement.

'It's him,' Melba said. 'The one I was telling you about.' She was balancing on one leg and massaging her damaged toes.

'So you're the chappie?' the sandy-haired man said. He looked Krippendorf up and down with unconcealed curiosity. 'I've been hearing all about you and your wee pickies.'

'Pickies?'

'Pictures, photographs. I expect you get a nice bob or two for them in Old Compton Street?'

Krippendorf drew himself up to his full height so that his head was practically touching the low plasterboard ceiling. 'I am afraid you have quite the wrong idea,' he said haughtily.

'Oh, I have quite the wrong idea,' said the man in a parody of a public school accent. He turned to Melba and leered. 'Has the gentleman come to take some more of you?'

Melba's eyes flashed. 'Don't you bloody start,' she hissed. 'I've had about enough with him.' She pointed melodramatically at the front door and jerked her chin at Krippendorf. 'Bugger off,' she said. 'And don't come back. I got a good mind to have you up before the Race Relations Board.' She shut the front door firmly behind him.

As he waited for the vandalized lift the sandy-haired man came strolling along zipping up his army-surplus parka. He dipped his head confidentially towards Krippendorf's. 'Did you really do that to her?' His voice was full of admiration.

'Do what to her?'

'Spray yoghurt over her tits and truss them up in your braces?'

Krippendorf looked away. 'I cannot discuss my work.'

The man winked, using every muscle in his face. 'You're on to a good number there, Jimmy. I reckon I could be of some assistance.'

Krippendorf let out an exaggerated sigh. 'I frankly doubt whether you have had any anthropological training.'

'Melba will do anything for me. I could easily get her to co-operate, if you take my meaning.' He narrowed his already narrow eyes. 'I'd want a percentage.'

'You obviously do not understand. I am engaged in purely ethnographic research.' He made no attempt to conceal his irritation.

'Call it what you like, Jimmy.' The man laughed his Scottish inner-city laugh. It sounded like a tin bath being dragged along a cinder track.

The lift door partially opened and Krippendorf squeezed in, trying to avoid the unidentifiable green slime on the walls and the fetid puddles on the floor. Before the door closed the man called out, 'If you change your mind, Jimmy, let me know. I can get the yoghurt for you wholesale.'

Five

'All right, all right, all right,' shouted Veronica, clapping her hands over her ears. 'Stop screaming all at once. Let's discuss it quietly and sensibly, one at a time. Shelley first.'

'Why should she be first?' Edmund whined. 'Just because she's a girl.'

'We ought to discuss who should speak first,' said Mickey. 'You're the one who's always saying we should be democratic among ourselves.' He was picking systematically at the white paintwork on the window frame, causing large flakes to fall on the shag-pile carpet.

Altering her tone to the didactic mode, Veronica said, 'Just *think* for a minute, Mickey. How could we possibly discuss the question of who should speak first? We'd have to decide who was going to speak first on *that* topic, and so on, and so on.'

Krippendorf coughed from behind his newspaper and turned to the sports pages. He was no longer astonished by his wife's attempts to treat the children as though they were rational human beings.

'We could draw straws,' suggested Edmund. He tore out another tuft of carpet, on which he was lying face down, and threw it into the empty grate. Fifteen minutes later, after a fierce argument over whether to draw straws, throw dice, or toss a coin, they drew straws. Shelley drew the longest straw and was allowed to speak first.

'I vote we go on a picnic. I mean a proper one with roast chicken in a hamper, and a white table-cloth, and knives and forks. Not the kind we usually have, with runny jam sandwiches and squashed plums.' She was inspecting herself in the mirror above the mantelpiece, assessing the compatibility of her platinum ear-studs with her Rastafarian dreadlocks. 'We could have it in that nice little wood near Stoke Poges where Jim-Jam had his heart attack.' They all laughed gleefully at the remembrance of it.

'It was merely indigestion,' Krippendorf said. He had read the sports news, the stock market prices, the court reports and the obituaries and was now absorbed in the special supplement on the Hungarian dry-cleaning industry.

'You made us call the ambulance,' Mickey reminded him. 'It was great. All those sirens going.' He made a passable imitation of a wailing siren and gouged out another flake of white paint with his powerful thumbnail.

'I vote we go to the transport museum,' Edmund said. Everybody groaned. 'Darling,' said his mother, 'it's too nice to go to a museum. It's the first sunny day we've had for ages.' She reached forward to extract a congealed grey substance from his hair. He pushed her hand away petulantly. 'I knew you'd say that. If it was wet you'd make a different excuse.'

'Darling, it's not an excuse, it's a reason. There's a big difference.'

'You always call your excuses reasons,' Edmund retorted. 'Just to make it sound better.' He had rolled over on his back and was now rhythmically kicking the doors of the rosewood drinks cabinet.

Mickey said, 'I say we go to the safari park.'

'Veto,' Krippendorf intoned from behind his crossword puzzle. He had solved all the clues containing anagrams and Shakespearian quotations and was now pondering over the identity of the erstwhile musical impresario whose wellington boots were thought to be unbecoming to the dissolute aunt of a lighthouse keeper (6,6).

'Why?' asked Mickey, in real or counterfeit surprise.

'Not after that last episode of yours when the car stalled among the lions. Edmund is fortunate to have retained the use of both arms.'

Mickey forced his thumbnail deep into the woodwork. 'No one in this house can take a joke,' he grumbled.

Shortly before noon the children clambered into the back of the car, already sweating and complaining. As they turned into the high street Shelley said, 'Why do we have to go to mouldy Brighton? I hate Brighton. What am I supposed to do there, build sandcastles?'

'Don't be such a misery,' Veronica said sharply. 'This is supposed to be a nice family treat. We don't often get the chance to do things together.'

'Whose fault's that?' Shelley mumbled, not quite inaudibly.

Veronica stared at her daughter in the driving mirror but made no reply. She was driving with both hands gripping the top of the steering wheel as though she would have preferred a faster car. The Sunday traffic to the coast was heavy and they were constantly stopping and starting. On the South Circular road they got stuck behind an articulated lorry with foreign numberplates. The sun beat down on the roof of the car, heating the fumes inside.

'I need a pee,' Edmund announced.

Veronica sighed, using her shoulders. 'Why didn't you pee before we left? I did ask you to.'

'I didn't need a pee then, I need it now.'

His mother put the handbrake on. 'Jump out then while we're stuck in this jam. And be quick.'

Edmund kicked his way past his brother and sister and began peeing against the rear wheel. The lorry in front suddenly moved forward and a moment later the charabanc behind hooted impatiently. 'For God's sake hurry up,' Veronica called. She drove forward very slowly with the rear door swinging open.

'Mummy, wait,' Edmund cried. He scampered awkwardly after the car, still peeing as he went. The knees of his trousers were wet and there were dark stains on his new Adidas trainers. Veronica stopped the car and he climbed quickly in, still dripping.

'Don't sit next to me,' Shelley said. 'You stink of piss, you disgusting little pig.' All three children then began elbowing, clawing and punching each other until Edmund burst into tears.

'Jamie,' shouted Veronica above the noise, 'could you *please* take your nose out of that road atlas and do something about the children. I am perfectly familiar with the route to Brighton. In any case,' she added, 'you've got it open at the Lake District.'

'Please be quite, children,' Krippendorf said amiably.

Veronica sounded her horn angrily at the car which had just cut across in front of them and whose four occupants were now leaning out of the windows waving beer bottles. 'Think of a game to play,' she said. 'Anything to shut them up while I'm driving.' Her face was damp and flushed and she blew periodically down the front of her open blouse.

Krippendorf shut the road atlas. 'Right,' he said. 'A quiz. There will be a prize for the contestant who has accumulated the greatest number of points by the time we have seen our third road accident starting from now.' He took a pound note from his wallet and held it up for the children to see. The screaming and fighting in the back quickly subsided and he waited until Edmund was able to retrieve his leg before commencing.

'First question, for five points: Name any tribe in sub-Saharan Africa whose kinship system is based on the principle of matrilateral cross-cousin marriage.'

The children shrieked in protest.

'Second question, for seven points,' Krippendorf said above the din. 'In not more than twenty-five words, and not repeating any word save for the definite and indefinite articles, explain the theory of surplus value.'

A collective howl of rage rose from the back seat. 'Ask us something we know about,' Mickey yelled. 'Like they do on Adolescent Brain of Britain.'

Krippendorf thought for a while. 'Very well, a Walt Disney question. Name any sixty of the One Hundred and One Dalmations.'

The children screamed hysterically and began kicking and hammering with their fists on the front seats. Veronica swerved the car into the side of the road and brought it to a shuddering halt. Still gripping the steering wheel at the top she rested her face on the backs of her hands. She seemed to be taking deep measured breaths like a pregnant mother practising enlightened childbirth. 'Jamie,' she gasped, 'I can't drive when the children are acting this way.'

Krippendorf looked at her with a puzzled frown. 'What way?'

'As they are now, of course.'

'Oh that,' he said jovially. 'That is not acting. That is their quite authentic and customary mode of behaviour.'

He drove the rest of the way to Brighton while Veronica pacified the children with sweets and the scatalogical version of I Spy.

Shortly after they arrived the weather changed. It began as a light shower and gradually developed into heavy rainfall. They sat huddled together around a table for two in a hamburger place filled with charcoal fumes. Rock music was thudding out from two large speakers on either side of them. Krippendorf could feel the heavy bass rhythms vibrating through the soles of his shoes. His legs were wedged tight beneath the tiny table and his smallest movement caused it to rise unsteadily off the floor like a table at a seance. After several attempts he caught the attention of one of the many waitresses dressed in short skirts and black stockings who hurried from table to table explaining the menu in educated accents.

Veronica ordered hamburger and chips for everyone.

'I'm not eating hamburger,' Shelley said.

'That's all they have. It's a hamburger restaurant.'

'I don't eat meat. I think it's disgusting.' She made a face designed to illustrate her sentiments.

Veronica said, 'But you're not a vegetarian.'

'Yes I am.'

'Since when?'

'I've been one for ages. Anyway, how would you know?'

Veronica glanced at her husband. 'Jamie, is this true?'

Krippendorf nodded in confirmation. 'She has been a vegetarian for at least eight, or possibly nine, days – with the partial exception of last Tuesday evening.' He looked at the blonde waitress and smiled without interest.

When the food came Shelley sat with her arms folded tightly across her chest, keeping bolt upright on her rustic wooden stool. She watched them biting into the scorched meat with ostentatious revulsion.

Edmund began to complain that Mickey was taking up more than his allotted half of their shared stool. A steady trickle of half-chewed food made its tortuous way down his chin and on to his Tottenham Hotspur tee-shirt. Krippendorf took a paper napkin and wiped at the pustules of tomato ketchup on his son's forehead. 'Edmund,' he said, 'let me explain to you once again the scientific principles of eating. The first fundamental point to grasp is that the food needs to be transferred from the plate to the mouth with a fork or a spoon or some equivalent instrument. This method renders it unnecessary to thrust the face forcibly into the plate as though it were a trough. Furthermore, it is not actually mandatory, in our advanced western culture, to rub the food into one's eyes, ears and hair. I realize that among certain Melanesian peoples this is indeed the custom, but only on ceremonial occasions as a mark of respect to one's host. Such courtesies are not really called for in the Brighton and Hove area.'

Edmund wiped the back of his hand across his mouth and said, 'When I've finished can I have forty pee for the Space Invaders?'

They waited for the rain to ease off a little before heading in the direction of the amusement arcade. They went in single file, with Veronica in the lead keeping close against the walls like soldiers in Belfast. On the way they passed groups of young men dressed in motor-cycle leathers walking four or five abreast along the narrow pavements. Policemen followed close behind them in twos, trying not to hurry. There was no evidence available to any of the senses of the nearness of the sea other than the squawk of a lone seagull circling above the multi-storey car-park.

Veronica changed a five pound note and distributed the coins equally among the children. Five minutes later they returned empty handed to ask for more. She persuaded them to play family bingo and they sat amongst elderly ladies in transparent plastic mackintoshes who had their own special bingo pencils. Mickey won a brass trinket with a crest on top that might have been a letter-holder or a toast-rack and which he tried unsuccessfully to exchange for a digital watch. Later they played the fruit machines and threw fluffy balls at a stack of tin cans without knocking any down.

'Can we go home now?' Edmund grizzled.

'No we cannot,' Veronica said. 'That's the third time you've asked in ten minutes. We've only just come.'

'We could go to the transport museum. You said we could go on a rainy day.' He was shivering in his damp tee-shirt and his hair was sticking up in wet spikes.

'No, darling, it would be shut by the time we got there.'

'I knew you'd say that,' he replied with grim satisfaction.

Veronica took his hand and led him briskly in the direction of the waxworks, calling for the rest of them to follow. She was determined to show that an enjoyable family outing could be had if they only put their minds to it.

The soft drizzle continued to fall. It eased off now and again just enough to raise false hopes. People dressed for a warmer and drier day stood beneath the dripping awnings looking up at the slate-grey sky and wiping their heads with their handkerchiefs. Already the day-trippers were straggling back up the hill on their way to the railway station. Some of them were laughing and joking as though cheered by the prospect of tea and toast in front of a blazing hearth. A light aircraft circled over the town trailing a banner advertising next week's flower carnival. It buzzed about quite low, disappearing and reappearing among the even lower clouds.

Two hours later Krippendorf stood watching it from the doorway of the sex shop that had been designated as the family assembly point. No one else had yet arrived and he toyed with the idea of going into the pub opposite and elbowing his way to the bar through what was certain to be a crowd of people in dripping mackintoshes.

As he was about to cross the road, Mickey appeared. He had his letter-holder or toast-rack in one hand and a corporation life-belt draped over his shoulder like a bandolier.

'Where did you get that?' Krippendorf demanded.

'I won it at bingo. You were there.'

'The other object.'

'I found it on the beach. It was just lying there.'

'That is exactly where it is meant to be.'

'No one was using it. It's just what I need for my new bathroom torture.'

'Take it back.'

'Oh, Dad, nobody's drowning.'

After a great deal of pleading and grumbling Mickey slouched away. While his father was still watching he took the lifebelt off and rolled it down the hill towards the sea.

Ten minutes later he returned accompanied by Edmund and Veronica. Edmund was trailing a helium-filled balloon that had partially collapsed. He looked tired and dispirited as he stamped through the puddles in his new Adidas trainers. There was no sign of Shelley.

'Are you certain you told her six o'clock?' Veronica said for the second time.

'Yes, fairly certain.'

'Just now you said you were absolutely certain.'

'Just now I was absolutely certain.'

He went twice round the block in search of her while Veronica waited with the boys in the doorway of the sex shop.

'Where the hell can the girl have got to?' she said on his return. She walked into the middle of the road and stared in both directions. 'Could she have gone straight back to the car?'

'She could have,' he said, 'assuming for example that I erroneously told her to be here at five instead of six.'

'James, you must surely *know* what you told her.' She often called him James when she was angry or upset.

'She was in that Greek place with that horrible food cooking in the window,' Mickey said. 'I saw her putting money in the juke-box.'

Veronica put her face very close to her son's. 'Well why didn't you say so before, you *silly* child.'

Mickey pointed at something in the brightly lit window of the sex shop. 'Because I was explaining to Edmund what those knobbly rubber things are for. He thought they were toy truncheons.'

Mickey led them down the hill to the little Greek café near the promenade. The bill of fare was written in whitewash across the window. A cylindrical slab of compressed meat was turning slowly on the spit next to the trays of stuffed aubergines and wrinkled peppers. Inside it smelled of hot stale fat.

Shelley was sitting at a table with a gang of boys who were dressed in almost identical leather jackets and heavy boots. She was puffing at a cigarette, holding it between the very tips of her fingers. She made no move to conceal it when she saw her mother.

'Shelley, what the hell do you think you're up to?' Veronica said. 'We've been waiting for you for *ages*. Can't you see the time?' She glanced around the café at the sweating walls and the ancient fly-paper hanging from the light-bulb. 'Put your shoes on this minute. Everyone's wet and tired.'

Shelley flicked her ashless cigarette over the saucerful of stubs in the centre of the table. Without quite looking at her mother she said, 'I'm not coming just yet.' She passed a box of matches to the boy sitting next to her.

Veronica took a pace forward and said in a clear, ringing voice, 'You heard what I said. Get your shoes on and put out that cigarette. *Now*.' She picked up Shelley's wet ballet shoes and tossed them on the table among the crash helmets and saucerless cups.

'You can go without me,' Shelley said. 'I've been offered a lift back.' She sucked in a mouthful of cigarette smoke and blew it all out at once, trying not to cough.

'You're doing nothing of the kind, my girl. You're coming back with me in the car.' Veronica's voice rose high above the falsetto from the juke-box singing monosyllabically about unrequited love.

'But it's all been arranged,' Shelley insisted. 'I'm going back with my friends.'

Something in Veronica seemed to snap. 'Will you stop talking such damned *non*sense. How can these people possibly be your friends?' She gave a comprehensively dismissive wave of the hand. At that moment the café proprietor emerged from behind an improbable bead curtain. He had an overflowing stomach that he lifted with both hands over the backs of the chairs like a man carrying a laundry bag. He slumped down, scratching himself through his string vest.

The youth sitting next to Shelley said, 'It's all right, missis, no need to worry. We'll take care of her.' He had a letter tattooed on each finger and a bronze crucifix around his neck.

'I'm not asking for your opinion,' Veronica snapped. 'She's coming home with me, she's only a child.'

'No, I'm not a child,' Shelley shouted. She stood up suddenly, causing her collapsible tubular chair to collapse. 'Jim-Jam doesn't mind if I stay, do you Jim-Jam?'

'I'm not interested in what your father thinks. I'm telling you, you're coming home with me this very minute.'

Shelley burst into tears. 'I'm not taking orders from you, you old cow. Whenever you come home you spoil everything. Why can't you just bugger off?' She pushed her way to the door and ran out into the street.

The youth with the tattooed fingers picked up his crash helmet and seemed about to follow in pursuit. Veronica seized hold of his arm. 'You just stay where you are,' she said. 'This is none of your concern.'

The youth pointed to his leather sleeve as though drawing attention to some flaw in its design or manufacture. 'You're holding my arm,' he said informatively. 'You shouldn't do that.' He shook his head in disappointment at her behaviour.

Veronica stepped back. The expression on her face changed from anger to alarm. 'James, don't just stand there,' she piped. 'What the hell are you doing?'

Krippendorf was leaning against the juke-box finishing off his crossword. He pencilled in the answer to seventeen across, an anagram of Goethe's big toe, and fastidiously refolded his newspaper. 'Could you put me in the picture?' he said. 'I seem to have lost track of events.'

Veronica half-stifled a scream. Closing her eyes, she

101

said in a strangulated voice, 'Your daughter has gone running off. Will you *please* go and find her. I've had about enough.'

The youth with tattooed fingers was buckling up one of his many straps. 'It's tanking down out there,' he remarked.

'That is absolutely right,' said Krippendorf.

'And she's got no shoes on,' the youth added.

'Right again. Though of course the fact of her shoelessness is not the sole or even principal reason for wishing to find her. Even on the supposition that she was adequately shod there would still be a strong case for . . .'

'James, for *Christ's* sake will you stop rabbiting and go and find her.' Veronica dragged Mickey forcibly away from the back of the juke-box, where he was doing something with a fork, and propelled him towards the door. 'I'll take the boys back to the car,' she said. 'Please be as quick as you can.'

Krippendorf turned up the collar of his linen jacket and made for the promenade. As he was passing the Maltese fish-and-chip shop the tattooed youth caught up with him. 'I'll come with you,' he announced. In his studded jacket and metal-capped boots he gave the impression of having more physical energy than he could lawfully employ.

Unexpectedly the rain had stopped, but the wind blowing from the sea had no drying qualities. Somewhere over the downs thunder rumbled. The youth offered Krippendorf a cigarette from a crumpled packet and Krippendorf surprised himself by taking one. Each time they came to a pizza parlour, pancake house, curry emporium or Szechuan take-away they stopped to look through the windows at the customers inside.

'In all probability we are doing the wrong thing,' Krippendorf said as they surveyed a party of Norwegian sailors seated around a table and chewing knobs of lamb on skewers. 'My daughter is a vegetarian at the moment.'

'You mean she don't eat meat?'

'That is correct,' Krippendorf said in a tone that suggested pleasurable surprise at his companion's powers of comprehension.

'Load a bollocks all that,' the youth said mildly. He revealed that he lived in Streatham with his demented mother and that he had been a trainee baths attendant before the redundancies. 'I nearly got a job last year in the glue factory in Clapham, but they closed it down the day I was meant to start.' He laughed good-humouredly and swung his crash helmet by the straps in a complete orbit.

It was already getting dark as they went down to the beach and began looking behind the stacks of deck chairs and under the upturned boats. The waves banged against the shore and somewhere out at sea a ship hooted.

'This is the place we had a right punch-up Easter before last,' the youth observed. 'It was an East End mob. I got stabbed in the neck.'

'I believe I saw it on the nine o'clock news.'

'They had wooden clubs with razorblades stuck in.'

'It was rather well done, I thought. At least, as a piece of reportage.'

'Them birds was a hard bunch. The things they done with their scissors.'

'It was hopelessly weak on analysis, of course. The parallels with Maasai warrior bands were completely overlooked.'

The youth stopped in his tracks. 'Hang about,' he said. 'Over there.' He pointed to a solitary figure near the water's edge.

Shelley was scooping up water in her cupped hands. 'They glow in the dark,' she said. Her straw-coloured dreadlocks were congealed in a wet tangle like pasta that had gone badly wrong. Krippendorf took off his damp linen jacket and draped it across her shoulders. She stood up and buried her face in his armpit as she used to do.

'I'll be off, then,' the youth said. When they could no

longer see him they could still hear the soft crunch of his boots on the wet shingle.

It was a long trek up the hill past the clock-tower to the car-park by the burned-out furniture depository. Shelley leaned against her father all the way. She managed to keep her arm around him by gripping the waistband of his trousers. His jacket came down well below her knees, giving the impression that she had nothing on beneath.

'Jim-Jam?' she said, in a tone he had learned to recognize.

'Mm?'

'You and the old cow, why haven't you got divorced?'

The road was practically deserted but they waited at the pedestrian crossing for the little green man to light up. 'Are you intimating we should?'

'I wouldn't mind if you did. I mean I wouldn't turn all peculiar and start pissing the bed.' He had forgotten to pick up her ballet shoes and her bare feet went slap slap on the road.

'Your mother and I would never be able to agree on custody of the children,' he said as he steered his daughter around something suspicious on the pavement. 'She would insist that I should have you all.'

As they were passing a row of discreetly lit massage parlours Shelley said, 'You ought to think about it. All my friends' parents are divorced or separated. It's not very nice being the odd one out.'

The car-park was unlit but they could make out the dark shape of the Volvo beyond the unauthorized rubbish tip. As they got nearer they could see the glow of Veronica's cigarette through the windscreen. 'Maybe she'll soon die of lung cancer,' Shelley said happily.

Six

Mickey's comprehensive school was a cluster of low buildings that looked as though they might once have been intended as temporary accommodation while the actual school was being built. At the rear was a misshapen sports field upon which children in shorts and singlets were now running about and screaming. A rubicund man in a tracksuit occasionally blew a whistle that hung around his neck on a ribbon. He trotted about sparingly in the very centre of the field shouting encouragement and abuse.

Krippendorf observed this activity from the other side of the buckled wire fence until it was time for his appointment. He ambled through the corridors, pausing once or twice to inspect the notice-boards. One of them carried a warning against further gross misuse of the bicycle sheds and another displayed blurred snapshots of the school trip to Nijmegen. There was a letter asking for volunteers to paint old people's homes and another requesting the return of the lollipop lady's missing lollipop.

The headmaster's study was at the end of a passageway adorned on either side with faded and talentless drawings of the same stately home. Precisely at the appointed hour Krippendorf knocked on the door, paused for the answering voice, and went in.

'Hi,' the headmaster said, advancing towards him with one arm fully extended. He enclosed Krippendorf's hand with both his own, causing Krippendorf to wonder whether he might be transmitting some arcane sign. 'Grab a pew,' he said, removing a pile of algebra texts from a chair and dusting the seat perfunctorily with the backs of his fingers.

'Thank you, headmaster.'

'Head teacher, actually. I always think headmaster sounds a bit Dickensian, don't you? This isn't exactly Dotheboys Hall, ha, ha.' He sat on the executive-style desk swinging his legs in the knee hole. He wore blue denim trousers that looked uncomfortably tight around the waist. 'It's good of you to come at such short notice. I don't think I've seen you since the school pantomime.' He held his legs out perfectly straight and knocked his ankle boots together.

'I was at the parents' meeting subsequent to that,' Krippendorf informed him, 'to discuss the social origins of the school riot.'

'So you were, so you were.'

'And again at the meeting called last March to deal with the outbreak of religious mania in 4B.'

'You were indeed,' said the head teacher, wagging a finger at him. 'As I recall, you had some novel proposals of your own for dealing with the problem.' He fiddled nervously with his bronze medallion before tucking it back inside his open-necked shirt. Quickly changing the subject he said, 'By the way, I've been meaning to drop you a line to thank you for the video recorder. It's terrific, just what we needed.'

'Video recorder?'

'The one you donated to the drama club. Mickey is in charge of special effects.'

'I see.'

'They're working very hard on the new production. It's an attempt to combine the earthiness and relevance of street theatre with the classical format of *son et lumière*.'

'Hm.'

'Our new drama teacher wrote the script himself. It's based on the Mau Mau rebellion. He believes in catering to the tastes of our ethnic constituency.' He ran a hand through his hair like a comb. His hair looked as if it had been styled rather than merely cut and could only just be described as prematurely grey. He chatted on amiably for a while about the recent stranglings in the boys' lavatories and the leprosy scare in the remedial class. A bell rang outside followed almost immediately by the sound of hundreds of feet clattering through the corridor. When the noise had died down enough to make conversation possible again he said, 'You've probably guessed why I asked you to drop in?' He propelled himself athletically off the desk and landed with his feet together.

'Something to do with Mickey, perhaps?' Krippendorf ventured.

The head teacher's youngish face became grave. 'I'm afraid so.' He opened a drawer in a steel filing cabinet and took out a dossier. It seemed to Krippendorf remarkably thick.

'As I think you know, we're a pretty easy-going bunch here. I don't believe in discipline for the sake of it. I like to give the kids a chance to express themselves in their own individual ways, to let them learn by their own mistakes. It's no use trying to stuff things into their heads. You've got to draw out what's already there.' He squeezed his outstretched hand around a ball of air and pulled it slowly towards his chest. 'That's the literal meaning of your word "education" – to lead out.' He opened the dossier and smoothed down the uncrumpled contents with his fist. Some of the papers were in the wrong order and he spent a minute or two rearranging them. Finally he said, 'You know, your lad Mickey puzzles me. He's a very unusual case.'

'Unusual?'

'As far as his work's concerned he's very together. He's got a very enquiring mind.'

'Hng.'

'But behaviourally he can be a bit of a problem. He upsets

a lot of the teachers. Some of them won't have him anywhere near their classrooms.' His tone was sorrowful rather than censorious. 'Please don't get me wrong. He's not one of your heavy brigade. As far as I know he doesn't even carry a knife.' He extracted a sheet of pink paper from the dossier and held it aloft for Krippendorf to see. 'This is a list of the complaints I've had about him this term.' He flapped the sheet of paper. Without referring directly to it he then began to recite the complaints in chronological order.

'April 4th. Reported for illicitly re-programming the school computer to erase Sociology from the curriculum.'

Krippendorf shrugged diffidently. 'I think he felt it was too heavily biased towards the positivist tradition.'

'April 17th. Discovered defacing the NUT strike banner.'

Krippendorf spread his hands. 'He is, I know, somewhat contemptuous of trade union consciousness. He regards it as petty bourgeois.'

'May 2nd. Reprimanded for making racialist remarks to the dinner ladies.'

'Mickey? Surely not?'

'He accused them of white imperialist bias in their distribution of the spotted dick.'

The head teacher read out several more indictments before replacing the sheet of pink paper in the dossier. 'I'm afraid it can't go on like this. The point has now been reached when I'm bound to take some action.' He went to the window and gazed out with apparent fascination at the high concrete wall immediately in front. Seen from behind he looked shorter and his trousers tighter still. As though reading a prepared statement he said, 'I'll have to put the Child Welfare people in the picture. That's the new policy in cases of this kind. They'll want to see if everything's OK on the home front.'

Krippendorf inclined his head thoughtfully. 'Well, well,' he said. 'The entry of Leviathan.'

'They'll probably send one of their bods around for a chat.

You know the sort of thing.' The head teacher smiled reassuringly with one side of his mouth. 'When kids start acting up it's often because of family troubles. I always say there are no problem kids, only problem parents. Though I'm sure that's not true in your case, ha, ha.'

Shelley was squatting cross-legged on the kitchen table stitching corporal's stripes on the arm of her Cuban battle fatigues. Without looking up she said, 'I'll need an increase in my pocket money soon.'

'You have just had an increase,' Krippendorf protested. 'It was in line with the Retail Price Index.'

'Yes, but I'll need extra.'

'Shelley, it was eight and a half per cent. That is more than the miners got.'

She sighed in a way designed to convey the futility of the entire cosmic order. 'Jim-Jam, try to think. I'm a girl. I'm thirteen.'

'I'm fully aware of both those demographic facts,' he said, just before the penny dropped.

'You can't expect me to buy tampons out of my sweet money.'

'Jamie, I don't intend to discuss it any further. We're getting a full-time housekeeper, and that is bloody well that.' Veronica screwed her eyes shut as she pulled the stiff brush through her thick auburn hair in a succession of swift strokes.

'A housekeeper?' Krippendorf said. 'A *housekeeper?*' His lips puckered in distaste, as though he were enunciating the name of a dog food or a trade union leader. 'I think you are over-reacting.' He was sitting on the edge of the bed trying to free his new shirt from its polythene wrapper, hidden pins, celluloid collar and expanded polystyrene cuff-protectors.

'I'm not over-reacting,' Veronica shouted. 'You heard as well as I did what that appalling little man said. Either we keep Mickey under control or they'll take him into care. They'd probably take all the children into care.'

Krippendorf removed a shred of polythene from his teeth. 'He was probably exaggerating. No credence can be given to a grown man who wears Scandinavian clogs.'

'Jamie, please try to be serious. He's the Principal-something-or-other in the Child Welfare Department. You heard him going on about all the statutory powers they've got. It's terrifying.' She stepped into a black-and-white knee-length dress and pulled up the zipper. Standing with her back to the oval mirror and looking over her shoulder, she said, 'Anyway, it's perfectly obvious that things can't go on as they are. You're just not up to taking care of the house and the children on your own. It's as simple as that.'

Krippendorf buttoned up his shirt. Veronica had bought it for him in a souk or casbah. It was tapered at the waist and tight across the shoulders, making him look unnaturally athletic. 'That is not a view everyone would endorse,' he said quietly.

'We can convert the guest room. It's just about big enough, and she'd be right next to Mickey.'

Krippendorf looked up. 'Who would?'

'The housekeeper, for Christ's sake.'

He gave a deep and protracted sigh. 'Veronica, do you quite realize what this would mean? A total stranger thrusting herself into the bosom of the family? It is against every human instinct. It is a violation of primordial moral boundaries, an assault upon the dignity and sanctity of domestic life. Anything that endangers the internal unity of the family threatens the very foundations of our civilization. Surely you know that?'

Veronica tugged violently at the crutch of her micro-mesh tights, as though attempting to catapult herself upwards. 'Jamie,' she intoned. 'We are talking about a housekeeper, not an airborne invasion by the Red Army.'

'She will never be able to adjust to our ways,' he protested.

'I should bloody well hope not. That's the whole point of having her – to *change* things around here.' Veronica forced her small foot into an even smaller shoe. 'Now please get a move on. The babysitter's here.'

When he set eyes on the babysitter his spirits immediately soared despite the prospect of having to spend three hours watching people standing about and talking on a stage.

'Where did you find her?' he asked Veronica as she swung the car recklessly into the high street.

'The Allenbys put me on to her. She's a student nurse or something.'

'Is she Ethiopian? She has that Pharaonic look they all seem to have.'

'I haven't the faintest idea. Why?' She turned her head to look directly at him while driving at high speed. She often did the same to passengers in the rear seat.

'Idle curiosity,' he said, closing his eyes to the oncoming juggernaut.

His thoughts about the babysitter made concentration on the play even more difficult than usual. It appeared to be about three people trapped in a lift, each of whom took it in turns to make long and thinly veiled speeches about the human predicament. Throughout the first act he fidgeted in his seat trying to dislodge a previously undetected pin from the collar of his new shirt that had now become embedded in his neck. Each time he raised his arm the woman in the seat behind hissed and Veronica jabbed him forcefully with her elbow. In the second act he got cramp in his leg, and in the final act the hurriedly eaten Mutton Vindaloo conducted a noisy assault upon his stomach. There were no drinks at

111

the interval because of the barmaids' strike against sexual harassment.

'What did you think of it?' Veronica asked on the way home.

The director was a close friend of hers so he refrained from saying that it was the best play about three philosophers stuck in a lift he had seen that month. Instead he said, 'The precarious edifice of neo-realism erected in the first act could support neither the heavy metaphysical load piled upon it in the second act nor the gratuitously surreal denouement, though I must say that the balance between existential pathos and *Entfremdungseffekt* was, with one or two minor lapses, delicately maintained. Would you agree?'

Veronica swerved sharply to avoid a stationary bus. 'How would you know?' she said. 'You were asleep through most of it.'

They drove the rest of the way home in silence. As they were going up the front steps Veronica tossed him the car keys. 'Will you drive the babysitter back, I'm knackered.'

He found the babysitter in the kitchen frying oven chips in a saucepan of smouldering fat. 'I make cooking for your little boy,' she said. 'He say me that every night at eleven you take him fried eggs and ships in bed.'

Krippendorf explained to her gently about Edmund. 'With the last babysitter it was pancakes and chocolate sauce,' he said, helping her off with her apron. She was taller than Melba and held her shoulders well back as though she might have been used to carrying things on her head. He had a quick vision of her re-stringing her bow, sharpening the points of her arrows and dipping them in curare. She would be a magnificent huntress, fleet of foot and deadly at the kill. Tomorrow he would get the appropriate materials.

In the car he leaned across and buckled up her seat-belt. She told him in halting English that she was from Addis Ababa where her father was something indecipherable in the service of the state. 'He was before a merchant in coffee, but we are socialist country now.'

Krippendorf sighed. 'Yes, it is a great pity. Such a fascinating country too. I very nearly did fieldwork there once, instead of Amazonia.'

'You spick my language?' she asked.

He shook his head as he changed gear, taking particular care to avoid touching her knee as he did so. Young women sometimes got the wrong idea.

'It is difficult for English people to spick. I try to titch them when I am in my country.'

'You gave lessons?'

'Yes, to help pay for studies.'

'Hm.'

A siren wailed behind them as they were passing the condemned housing estate. Krippendorf pulled into the side to allow the police car to pass. It sped by followed by two truckloads of soldiers dressed in riot gear.

'What is happening?' the babysitter asked.

'Oh, nothing very much. It is probably just another bread riot. Camden Town I should imagine, they are due for one about now.'

Five minutes later they pulled up outside a nurses' hostel. Reggae music blared from an open window unaccompanied by any redeeming sounds of Caribbean gaiety. Krippendorf took out his wallet and handed the babysitter several pound notes.

'This money is too much,' she protested weakly.

'My wife would wish you to have it.' He got out of the car and walked quickly round to open her door. She put both legs out at once and levered her body forward in a single elegant movement. While she was fumbling for her key he said, 'A thought has crossed my mind. Could you be persuaded to give some lessons in your native tongue?'

'Language lessons?'

113

'Precisely. Say two or three times a week, at your convenience?'

A little to his surprise she agreed at once. She also complied with his wish to pay her for the first month's tuition in advance. They arranged a time for the first lesson. 'I am sure you will enjoy it,' he said. 'It will be a lot more creative than babysitting.'

Driving back home with the car radio playing a lively gavotte Krippendorf's thoughts progressed from the matter of language lessons to the problem of language itself. Linguistic theory had been greatly advanced in recent years by the contributions from his own discipline. Only the other day he had read a learned article in the *Humberside Journal of Biosocial Studies* that had shown quite conclusively that body language was used more frequently, and to more telling effect, than verbal language among a scientifically selected sample of white urban rugby supporters. Scholars in the field were now engaged in a desperate race to see who would be first to decode the hidden grammar of non-verbal discourse. As he drove through the ill-lit and unswept streets he began to dwell upon Shelmikedmu language and its peculiarities. It would be most uncharacteristic, he thought, if their practices did not yield new and vivid insights into the problem.

He closed the front door quietly, removed his shoes, and crept up to his study. As he passed the master bedroom he heard Veronica snoring irregularly into her pillow. He lit a small cigar and made himself comfortable at his desk.

Language and Praxis: Notes on Verbal and Non-Verbal Modes of Interpersonal Discourse

In the transaction of everyday affairs Shelmikedmu communicate with each other through the medium of two quite separate types of language. One of them is verbal, and has some linguistic affinity to other indigenous tongues of Amazonia. The other is a form of body language that is wholly unique to the Shelmikedmu. These two different modes of discourse are often used simultaneously, in a complementary manner. For example, in Shelmikedmu the terms 'yes' and 'no' are not differentiated at the verbal level; the selfsame word *prhxqo* is used to denote both expressions. This does not, however, result in any confusion or ambiguity because the utterance of the word *prhxqo* is always accompanied by a bodily gesture that renders its meaning clear. If the speaker wishes to give the word a negative connotation he draws his upper lip over his teeth while saying it, at the same time dilating his nostrils and rolling his eyes in a clockwise direction. If he wishes to give the word a positive meaning he thrusts his tongue into his lower lip while forcing his chin into his chest.

Shelmikedmu claim with some justification that this combination of verbal and non-verbal usages endows their language with great richness and flexibility. This may be shown especially in cases where exact quantities or measurements need to be expressed. If an Englishman is asked at the dinner table how much roast beef he would like, or if an Italian is asked how much spaghetti he wants, he can only answer in the vaguest terms: a small helping, a large helping, or a medium helping. And these imprecise terms are rendered even less exact by dint of the differing conceptions that people have of what constitutes a large, small or medium helping.

A Shelmikedmu experiences no such difficulties. He can reply with great precision when asked how much tapir hot-pot or paw-paw crumble he would like. In addition to uttering the word for, say, a large helping (*mqlux*) he will simultaneously distend his stomach to one of the eight recognized positions or degrees, each of which represents the exact quantity of foodstuff required.

The combination of verbal and body language has very wide application. When Shelmikedmu sit around gossiping and arguing, their talk is always interspersed with the animated cocking of legs, heaving of shoulders and gyrating of necks. Indeed, when matters become heated, or finer points of debate are being raised, complete silence may fall as the crudities of verbal exchange are completely abandoned in favour of the subtleties of body discourse.

When darkness falls, and the nuances of facial and physical gestures are less easy to perceive, aural forms of non-verbal discourse come into their own. Shel-mikedmu have developed over the centuries a refined vocabulary of body sounds. Without a word being spoken they can converse freely in the dark by cluck-ing, whistling, cheeping, snorting, gurgling, belching and breaking wind. Shelmikedmu have exceptionally well-developed diaphragm and sphincter control essen-tial for certain of their non-verbal utterances.

Krippendorf continued writing until the church clock struck one of the hours between two and five. As he climbed into bed Veronica mumbled something in her sleep. That night he dreamt of running through a thick forest, pursued by men with sharp sticks. He fell to the ground and a pair of cold hands gripped him by the throat. 'Jamie, Jamie, for Christ's sake,' Veronica said. She was sitting up in bed pushing hard against his chest. 'You've woken me up three times with your noise.' She reached across for the bedside clock. 'I've got to get up at six. How can I get any sleep with you babbling in my ear about witchcraft substances?'

Mickey's face was like a crumpled paper bag. 'I don't want to learn Amharic,' he whined. 'I don't even know what it is.'

'I have just explained. It is a foreign language.'

'I'm already learning French, that's bad enough.' He picked abstractedly at a loose corner of the dark green patch that his father had recently glued over the hole in his brown school blazer.

'This is quite different. This is a language spoken by the people of what used to be the Kingdom of Ethiopia but is now most probably the People's Democratic Republic.'

'That's in Africa.'

'Correct. It is time you extended your cultural horizons.'

'What's the use of learning the language if I'm not going there?'

Krippendorf scraped at deposits of coagulated gravy on the sandwich toaster with a pair of scissors. 'You can never be certain of that. It is as well to be prepared for all contingencies.'

'I'll bet it's a hard language to learn.'

'Must you always be so negative? Try to look upon it as an intellectual challenge.' He began collecting small scraps of cheese off the kitchen table and from beneath the chairs and wrapping them individually in squares of tinfoil. He then put them in the refrigerator alongside other similarly wrapped and disregarded leftovers. Eventually, when they had turned unambiguously mouldy, he would throw them all away. 'I was contemplating buying you a decent cricket bat,' he said non-committally.

Mickey's widely spaced eyes flickered into life. 'If I learn Amharic?'

'If you agree to have lessons. I know of an excellent teacher.'

Mickey thought for a moment. 'I'd rather have another airgun.'

'I think not. We are still suffering from the repercussions of the first.'

117

Mickey folded his arms. 'Airgun,' he said in a firm monotone.

Krippendorf did some rapid moral arithmetic. 'Very well. Let it be an airgun.'

'Foreign, not British?'

'Naturally.' He gathered up an armful of dirty dishes and stacked them haphazardly in the sink. 'Your first lesson is tomorrow. The teacher will be here at three-fifteen.'

'Three-fifteen? You know I don't get home from school till four.'

Krippendorf smiled privately. 'I dare say we shall be able to fill the void.'

'This is where my wife has elected to put you,' Krippendorf said morosely as he opened the door of what had previously been the guest room. 'As you can see, it is incommodious in the extreme. The ceiling is in danger of collapse, and there is a rats' nest beneath the rotting floorboards.'

Mrs Guntrip held her handbag in both hands as she surveyed the room from the doorway. 'Very pleasant,' she said. 'Nice and airy, just like Mrs Yardley said.' She had a small round face perched unstably upon a small round body, as though in imitation of a child's first rough attempt at a plasticine figure.

Krippendorf made an apologetic gesture. 'Even in the mildest winter the temperature falls to sub-zero. Our guests suffered cruelly from hypothermia.'

Mrs Guntrip took a couple of tentative steps into the room. She gave the impression of someone walking across a floor that was still being washed. Standing well away from the bed, she pressed the mattress ineffectually. 'Lovely springing,' she declared in a voice whose cadences and accent he took to be Welsh.

'I dare say Mrs Yardley alerted you to the problem of the

noxious fumes that seep through the leaking radiator pipes?'

Mrs Guntrip went to the window and touched the curtain. 'There's pretty,' she said. 'I do like a bit of pink in a bedroom.'

Krippendorf's voice rose in alarm. 'Never stand in front of the window. On account of the crazed SAS marksman holed up in the house opposite.'

Mrs Guntrip stared at him as though trying to recognize him from an old photograph. 'Pardon? Were you saying something, Mr Yardley? You'll have to speak up a bit, my batteries are running down.' She undid the top button of her latex-foam overcoat and tapped lightly on the small microphone connected by a wire to a plug in her ear.

Krippendorf pulled thin pieces of skin off the ends of his fingers and rolled them into a ball. 'A fat, deaf, Welsh housekeeper,' he muttered disbelievingly.

'I'll start on Monday week, like I promised,' she said. 'I've heard such a lot about the children from Mrs Yardley, I can hardly wait to meet them.'

Seven

Shelley was thawing out a slab of frozen mince under the hot water tap. She had meant to take it out of the freezer before going to school, but had become absorbed in the unmarried mothers' panel game on breakfast television. It was the only breakfast programme that she watched, apart from the psychosomatic phone-in and the dolphin serial.

When the mince had turned fairly soft and grey on the outside she dropped it in a frying pan over a high flame. Presently she began peeling onions and chopping them with a noisy mechanical gadget. The kitchen quickly filled with smoke and steam.

She put her head outside the door and shouted upstairs, 'Jim-Jam, how much spaghetti do you want?' There was no reply and she repeated the question. Almost at once her father came heavily down the stairs looking distraught.

'What was it you said?' he asked in a curiously shaking voice.

'I'm making Spaghetti Bolognese. How much do you want? The water's boiling.'

Krippendorf took a pace towards his daughter and looked at her accusingly. 'Have you been reading my confidential papers? I have asked you never to enter my study without permission.'

Shelley wiped the perspiration off her nose with the Coronation tea-cloth. 'What are you on about? D'you want any spaghetti or not?'

Krippendorf struggled to bring his voice under control.

'Shelley, just reflect for a moment. What could possibly constitute an informative reply to the question, "How much spaghetti do you want?"'

'Jim-Jam, are you feeling all right? You look a bit funny.'

'Just answer me. It is a matter of some importance.'

Shelley raised a greasy spatula and slapped it hard against the leg of her Bolivian Air Force trousers. 'Look, just tell me if you want a big helping or a little helping. The last time I had to throw most of it away.'

Krippendorf put his hands on his hips. 'And how, precisely, would you translate my request for, let us say, a little helping, into concrete action? It must surely have occurred to you that the expression "little helping" is far too imprecise to designate a specific quantum of spaghetti. Do they teach you nothing at that school?'

'If you're going to be like that you can get your own dinner,' Shelley pouted. She watched in amazement as her father first drew in his stomach and then let it slowly inflate. 'There you are,' he said, revolving his eyes as he pointed to the tight bulge beneath his slimfit shirt. 'That is exactly how much spaghetti I want.'

A day or two later Shelley called him into her bedroom as he was passing with the Ali Baba laundry basket. She pointed to a purple stain on the sheet. 'Look, it's happened.'

He bent down to inspect it. It was roughly the shape of a badly drawn map of Cyprus. He let out a small cry of exaltation. 'We must have a celebration.' He removed the sheet from the bed and folded it with care, like a regimental flag.

'Celebration?' Shelley stood with her legs apart, holding her cotton nightshirt away from her body.

'A menarche celebration,' her father explained. 'Your transition to puberty must be marked by an appropriate *rite de passage*.'

'A party you mean? None of my friends had one. They all hushed it up.'

'Not a party in the conventional sense. More of an exclusive kinship ceremony. At times like this the family transcends its internal contradictions and reaffirms the bonds of social solidarity and moral unity.'

'We could all go out to Burgerland.'

Krippendorf gave an exasperated sigh. 'Shelley, try to appreciate the gravitas of the event. Yesterday you were a child, today you are a young woman. Such an occasion cannot be dignified by the consumption of hamburgers and chips.'

'I don't feel any different, apart from the mess.'

Krippendorf laid a fatherly hand upon his daughter's shoulder. 'All the more reason for us to enlist the aid of collective social sentiments to instil the proper sense of awe.'

Immediately after breakfast he went to the street market and bought sweet potatoes, mangoes, coconuts, Chinese gooseberries and green bananas. He spent the rest of the morning peeling, scraping, pounding, chopping, frying and boiling. Later he baked a loaf of unleavened bread and a tray of small rice cakes. After the food had been prepared he drove to the Punjab Emporium and made several expensive purchases with his American Express card.

By the time Edmund and Mickey returned home from school most of the preparations were complete. He made them bath at once in water perfumed with one of the new commercial brands of frankincense. After some instinctive grumbling they allowed themselves to be drawn into the occasion, intrigued by this unexpected departure from routine. He got them to wash their hair with herbal shampoo, scrub their teeth with menthol toothpaste, and to have their toenails clipped. He then set out the white smocks and rope sandals he had bought for them in the emporium. From his bedroom he could hear them whispering and giggling as they buttoned up their smocks.

'Why are the curtains drawn in the living-room?' Edmund asked.

'So that the candlelight looks better, stupid.'

'What was that funny smell?'

'It's called incest. They burn it in church.'

'What's it all for, anyway?'

'It's for Shelley. Don't you ever listen?'

'Her birthday's not till after mine.'

'It's nothing to do with birthdays, stupid. It's because she's a girl.'

'That's not fair.'

'From now on she can have babies whenever she likes.'

'Ergh, that's disgusting. They make us watch films about all that at school.'

Krippendorf completed his own elaborate toilet and changed into ceremonial clothes. He knocked on Shelley's bedroom door and went in. He had given her the day off school and she had spent most of the time in her room practising her electric guitar. 'Everything is now ready,' he said. 'I should like you to put this on.' He held out the sari.

'Why must I wear that?' she said, pulling a face. 'I don't like the colour.'

'It has to be red and white for obvious symbolic reasons.'

She ran her fingers along it. 'What sort of material is it?'

'It is pure silk, imported from the east.'

She held the sari against her thin, angular body. Despite his hurried needlework it was still a little too long.

'It looks funny.'

'Shelley, it is for a brief ceremony only. As soon as it is over you can get back into your insulation lagging.'

She hovered perceptibly on the brink.

'All right then.'

He had shifted all the living-room furniture into one corner and rolled back the shag-pile carpet. Across the now bare floorboards lay a length of the frayed straw matting that he sometimes used in his photographic work. At the side of this was a low table covered with a black velvet cloth on which he had set out bone-china plates and dishes containing fried green bananas, mashed sweet potato, mango slices with ginger, rice cakes, unleavened bread and a bowl of chilled coconut milk. In the centre of the table three candles flickered in a tall silver candlestick. On the floor at each side of the table was an old car cushion neatly encased in a clean white pillowslip. Incense sticks were burning on the drinks cupboard in a darkened corner of the room and the sonorous tones of Bach's *Toccata and Fugue in D minor* issued from a cassette recorder concealed beneath a damask cloth.

The children entered the room slowly, in single file, and stood by their appointed car cushions until their father motioned for them to be seated. Before taking his own seat he went from one to the other offering plates of food. He hovered and flapped above them like a great mythological bird in his flowing black kimono and scarlet tennis headband. Edmund and Mickey exchanged glances as they bit cautiously into their mango and ginger slices. Edmund held his hand under his chin to catch the drips. Neither of them dared to giggle. Shelley made a small adjustment to her sari. She had taken an immediate liking to it as soon as her father had fitted it on her in front of the long oval mirror. She sipped her chilled coconut milk demurely, conscious of being the centre of attention. No one spoke.

How different his children were, Krippendorf thought,

when they were under the benevolent spell of powerful ritual forces. How right Durkheim was about the transformative effect of high ceremony upon the individual psyche. While the collective moral energy was still at its peak he gave two solemn handclaps, cleared his throat, and proceeded to deliver his prepared homily.

'In all known cultures, my children, there are certain days in the life-cycle that are set apart from others and treated as sacred, in the broadest sense of that term. In western civilization, as you all know, we celebrate a person's birth, marriage and death by performing certain joyful or sober ceremonies. But strange as it may seem we do not accord social recognition to what is arguably the most crucial event of all in the human calendar: the onset of puberty. The passage from girlhood to womanhood is not merely denied social acknowledgement, it is actively concealed as though it were a matter for shame. In many other cultures a far more healthy attitude prevails. The occasion is treated with open rejoicing and festivities lasting for several days among peoples as diverse as the Iroquois, the Maoris, and the Shelmikedmu.

'Now, it is obvious that all rituals and all ceremonies have to begin somewhere and with someone for the first time. I see no reason why an English menarche ceremony should not originate with us here and now in this very room. From our modest beginnings great things may follow. We could today be planting a small seed that will eventually grow in the popular consciousness and spread its roots across the land. A time may come, in the not too distant future, when Menarche Day will be celebrated with the same pride and gaiety that now attends other happy occasions. It is by no means impossible that even in your own lifetime young women, on their transition to puberty, will be serenaded to the strains of "Happy Menarche to You". In future years, pubescent women will very likely wear badges or colourful tee-shirts to proclaim their new socio-biological status. W.

H. Smith's will stock menarche greetings cards of the sentimental, flippant, and scurrilous variety. The possibilities are endless.

'Much depends, of course, on the readiness of the Royal Family to take a lead. The ceremony would very quickly become established if the King could be persuaded to announce the pubescence of the young princesses, in the manner of the Ashanti kings. Guns could be fired in Hyde Park to herald the good news. The princesses' bedsheets could be draped over the balcony at Buckingham Palace for all loyal subjects to see. Royal Menarche Day could be declared a public holiday. There could be fireworks displays at Alexandra Palace, street parties in the slums, outside broadcasts from Trafalgar Square . . .'

Krippendorf's face shone excitedly in the candlelight as he expanded upon his theme. He sat very upright, with his legs crossed, so that his black kimono was stretched tight across his knees. He gripped his ankles firmly above his grey deodorized socks. The toccata and fugue ended with a loud click just before he drew his peroration to a close. When he had finished it was completely silent except for the sound of Edmund breathing through his open mouth.

Krippendorf took two Tesco's blood oranges from a bowl on the table and sliced them dramatically in half with a machete. He then squeezed the juice into three wooden bowls, keeping one for himself and passing the others to his sons. He raised his bowl and cried aloud, 'To Shelley's menarche!' then swallowed the liquid in a single draught, together with the pips. Edmund and Mickey followed suit, while Shelley sat with her head slightly bowed.

'That concludes the ceremony,' Krippendorf announced. He snuffed out the candles and wet the tips of the incense sticks. As soon as the curtains were pulled back Edmund and Mickey scuttled out of the room holding their white smocks above their knees. Seconds later they were laughing and fighting on the stairs.

'Shelley,' he said, 'I have made up a bed for you in the garden shed. You will find it quite comfortable.'

'The shed? What for?' She was scrutinizing a strip of fried green banana as though wondering what she might have eaten in the semi-darkness.

'You obviously cannot sleep in the house for the next three nights, you do realize that?'

'Why not, what's wrong with my bedroom?'

'Nothing is amiss with your bedroom. The matter concerns yourself.'

'What have I done?' she protested shrilly.

'It is not a question of what you have or have not done. It is what you have become.'

'You mean my . . . thingy? That's not my fault.'

Krippendorf took his daughter's hands in his own. 'It is not a punishment. All menarche ceremonies culminate with the seclusion of the celebrant. You are now in a state of dangerous ritual impurity. You could bring great misfortune on us all if you do not follow the prescribed procedures.'

'None of my friends had to sleep in the garden.'

'Shelley, they are not like us.'

'The shed's full of spiders.'

Krippendorf allowed his eyes to close for a moment. 'Spiders? How can you talk of spiders when I am presenting you with an opportunity to make cross-cultural history?'

When the front door bell rang Krippendorf had his head in the gas oven. He was scraping at bits of jam roly-poly and the charred remains of Edmund's nylon underpants with the handle of a spoon.

Mrs Guntrip stood with one foot on the doorstep. She had an overflowing shopping bag in each hand and a collapsible umbrella tucked beneath her arm.

'Yes?' Krippendorf enquired. He stared at her as though she were selling clothes-pegs or soliciting support for the clergymen's strike.

'I've just brought my necessaries for now,' she said. 'I'll get the rest sent later.' She walked past him and went straight upstairs to her room.

'There is still time to reconsider,' Krippendorf called after her. 'Besides, we have seventeen other applicants to interview. It is a highly sought-after post.'

He returned from the public library later that afternoon to find the house smelling of pine disinfectant and wax furniture polish. Long-familiar food stains had been wiped off the kitchen walls, and the dishes had been properly washed and dried and put away in the wrong places.

Mickey intercepted him on the landing. 'Who's that old bag upstairs?' he whispered, jerking his thumb repeatedly over his shoulder.

'I presume you have met Mrs Guntrip. She has been sent to care for us all.'

Mickey's whisper gave way to an incredulous squeak. 'Is she bonkers or something? D'you know what she did?'

Krippendorf waited to be told.

'She inspected our teeth and our ears and our fingernails before giving us tea, and then she made Edmund say grace.'

'I am surprised Edmund's Latin was up to it.'

'During tea, she sent Shelley out of the room for farting. She said girls aren't supposed to fart.'

'Evidently she has replaced the batteries in her hearing aid.'

The stairs above began to creak and then Edmund's worried face appeared between the banister rails. He scuttled quickly down, as though being pursued.

'Has she gone?' he asked, clutching his father's sleeve.

'Not yet,' Krippendorf said. 'That is, if you are referring to whom I think you are referring.'

Edmund looked up into his father's face. 'What's she

doing here, bossing us about? She says I'm not to practise snorkelling in the bidet.'

Krippendorf stroked his son's matted hair. 'Your mother feels we are in need of help. She did try to explain to you the advantages it would bring.'

Edmund looked puzzled. 'I don't remember.'

'You were engrossed in the vampire musical.'

Mickey was pulling at a loose strip of the William Morris wallpaper and winding it around his finger. 'Is she foreign?' he asked. 'I can hardly make out a word she's saying.'

'Yes,' Krippendorf confirmed. 'She is Welsh. They are a stunted, plebeian race with socialistic tendencies. They sing collectively.'

Again the stairs above began to creak. Mrs Guntrip appeared wearing a blue nylon housecoat and fluffy carpet slippers with yellow pom-poms.

'There's lucky, Mr Yardley,' she said. 'I was hoping to find you.'

Krippendorf breathed slowly in and out. 'Our meeting is not wholly due to chance, Mrs Guntrip. I am quite often to be found standing or sitting in this general vicinity.'

She handed him a sheet of deckle-edged notepaper covered on both sides with a jagged script that looked as though it might have been written while she was riding pillion in a motor-cycle race. 'It's a list of the necessities I'll be needing for the children,' she explained. 'Mrs Yardley said I was to ask for anything pertaining to the carrying out of my duties.'

Krippendorf ran his eye down the list.

'Flea powder?' he said. 'Carbolic soap? Pumice stone?'

'No special hurry,' Mrs Guntrip informed him. 'Anytime tomorrow would do.' She suddenly noticed Edmund and Mickey hiding behind their father. 'Be off, you boys,' she said, giving three claps with her plump hands. 'Up to your rooms. One thing I can't abide is children loitering on the stairs.' She bustled past them, patting her almost invisible hairnet.

Krippendorf turned over the sheet of notepaper. 'Mrs Guntrip?' he called to her retreating back. 'Why do we need dandelion and burdock? And enema pessaries? And essence of ragwort?'

She disappeared into the kitchen without responding.

'Mrs Guntrip?' He hurried down and succeeded in manoeuvring himself in front of her just before she could reach the sink. He addressed himself directly to the bulge of her concealed microphone. 'Why do we need all these medicaments? They are not readily available under socialized medicine.' He held the list up in front of her to avoid ambiguity.

'That's right, Mr Yardley,' she nodded. 'We'll be needing all these things. You see, children's insides need a thorough weekly clean-out. You have to flush out all the toxic wastes and poisonous fluids that cause them to misbehave. Mark my words, you'll see how quickly their manners will improve.'

The weather grew warm and sometimes the sun shone for two or three days at a time. Soon people began to complain about the heat and about the smell of the uncollected garbage in the streets. Fresh pension riots broke out in Haywards Heath and Brize Norton and, despite the brain damage scare, long queues formed at the ice-cream stalls. Daily messages were broadcast over the radio advising elderly people how to avoid dehydration and a man from Lyme Regis was sent to prison after watering his garden on the wrong day of the week.

The sun was shining now through the large fanlight in Krippendorf's study, supplementing the heat and the light of the overhead lamps. 'Are we nearly finish?' the Ethiopian babysitter said. 'My arms are getting tiresome.'

'Tired,' he corrected her. 'Just one or two more and we

shall be done.' He shifted the tripod a few inches closer to where she was squatting on the floor binding a length of raffia around the sharpened end of a bamboo stick. Behind her, covering one complete wall of his study, was a blown-up picture of a small hut at the edge of a clearing in the rain forest.

'Could you scowl a little,' he said. 'A Shelmikedmu huntress looks very ferocious.' He demonstrated the facial effect he wanted. 'Excellent. Hold it just like that.'

He was recording scenes in the life of a typical spearwoman for the *Exotica* special edition on female aggression. She looked very much the part, he thought, wearing nothing but a leather thong around her tiny waist and five wooden rings from Edmund's hoopla dangling around one ankle.

'There we are,' he said on a note of triumph, 'all done. You were very, very good.'

The Ethiopian babysitter stood up and stretched her arms and legs. She had long legs on quite a short but slender body. Her breasts pointed upwards and outwards, growing away from each other like two separate entities rather than a single bosom. 'Chames?' she asked, 'why do you make these pictures?'

'It is part of my research. I do not wish to bore you with the ethnological details.'

She sat on the divan and began massaging her legs below the knees. An electric fan blew cool air across the room. The previous time she had complained about the heat. 'Shall I take these off?' she said, raising her leg and rattling the wooden hoopla rings.

'I think so. Edmund may need them for his own purposes.'

She reached out her hand. 'You must help me,' she said coyly.

Krippendorf slid the rings off her ankle one by one in what he assumed to be a detached and businesslike manner.

She patted the divan, inviting him to sit beside her. He looked demonstratively at his watch and said, 'Good lord, time is getting on. I have a banana sponge trifle to make.'

The babysitter bowed her head and said sadly, 'You do not want to love me. You do not like me, except for making pictures.'

Krippendorf shifted his weight from one foot to the other. 'Of course I like you. How could I not like you? You are the ideal Shelmikedmu huntress.'

'I am Ethiopian.'

'I like you irrespective of your ethnic identity.'

She kept her eyes fixed on the oblong strip of frayed straw matting. 'If you do not want to lie down with me anymore I cannot make pictures with you.'

Krippendorf sighed heavily and took his clothes off.

She took his maggot in her hand and closed her slender fingers around it, firmly but gently, as though it were a captive bird. Presently she looked up at him and smiled. 'You do still like me,' she said.

He lay beside her on the divan.

'Chames?' she said shyly, fingering the leather thong around her waist.

'Mm?'

'Can we love in the Shelmikedmu way? You promise me we can one day.'

'Did I really?'

'You say when your back is better.'

Krippendorf removed one of her hairs from his mouth. 'Not today. I do not have all the right facilities.'

The divan was on casters and soon began to slide across the room. She jumped about beneath him and made noises like an asthmatic running for the last bus. It seemed to go on for a very long time as Krippendorf mulled over the alternative titles for his forthcoming article on the couvade. Towards the end she gave a series of high gurgling cries, rising to a fierce and prolonged crescendo. 'Could you

132

please be a little quieter?' he whispered. 'Mickey is trying to learn his irregular Amharic verbs.'

While she was dressing he took an electric kettle from the bottom drawer of his filing cabinet and made two mugs of instant coffee. She hummed contentedly to herself as she unravelled her panties from her tights and put them on. Krippendorf noted without interest that she wore her panties over rather than under her tights. She looked around suddenly, surprised by the sound of someone hammering weakly on a door below.

'It is only Mrs Guntrip,' Krippendorf assured her, looking at his watch. 'Her sedative seems to have worn off prematurely. Next time you come I shall have to increase the dose.'

Shelley was lying face down on her bed throwing darts at a recognizable caricature of Mrs Guntrip chalked on her wardrobe door.

'Why can't you just tell her to bugger off, Jim-Jam?' she said, flinging a dart accurately at the smaller and uppermost of the two representational circles.

'Alas, it is not quite that simple. Your mother, among others, is convinced we are in need of her stabilizing presence.'

Shelley closed one eye and took aim. 'The old boot's really got it in for me. The other morning she deliberately emptied her pisspot over the marijuana seedlings in my windowbox.'

Krippendorf ducked as a dart bounced off the wardrobe door and flew towards his face.

'And now,' Shelley continued, 'she's jabbed a hole in my diaphragm with her knitting needle. If I get pregnant again it'll be all her fault.'

The telephone rang and Krippendorf hurried down to answer it.

Mrs Guntrip was there before him. 'Who? What?' he heard her shouting.

'Let me take it, Mrs Guntrip,' he called from the landing.

'No, I keep telling you,' she bellowed into the mouthpiece. 'There's no one here called that.' She slammed the receiver down before he could get there.

'Who was it, Mrs Guntrip? I am expecting an urgent call.' He bent down to her microphone and repeated the question.

'Wrong number, Mr Yardley. They were asking for some foreign gentleman. That's the third time today. I've a good mind to report it to the police.'

Krippendorf contemplated the bright yellow pom-poms on her carpet slippers and the folded copy of *Psychic News* protruding from the pocket of her blue nylon housecoat. 'According to the appointments columns of *The Times*,' he said, 'there are unlimited opportunities for qualified housekeepers in the United Arab Emirates. You could quickly save enough to retire in comfort to a pit village in Ebbw Vale. I have taken the trouble to cut out the advertisement.'

Mrs Guntrip watched him attentively as he spoke, reading the movements of his lips.

'Yes,' she smiled, 'I'll be serving supper in a jiffy, Mr Yardley. As soon as I've given Mickey his seaweed rub.'

Eight

Krippendorf lay in the bath, gripping the water taps with his long prehensile toes. His hair and eyebrows were smothered in a new shampoo that claimed to attack dandruff while repairing split ends. It crackled in his ears as he turned the damp pages of his espionage novel. It had lately been revealed that the corpse found buried beneath the goalmouth in Wembley Stadium was the illegitimate half-brother of the man with the artificial leg who had kidnapped the nun in the Dordogne. It further transpired that the nun herself was either the brains behind a plot to smuggle bibles into Cuba or the runaway mistress of a milk tycoon. Krippendorf checked the number of each page to make certain he had not turned two by mistake.

Mickey came bursting into the bathroom, followed by a gust of cold air.

'Go away,' his father said. 'Use the downstairs lavatory.'

'You'd better come quickly, it's Edmund.'

'I am taking my bath. You know full well that I do not deal with emergencies before five o'clock.' Shampoo had worked its way into his eyes and he groped blindly for the face-flannel submerged somewhere beneath the sandalwood-and-jasmine foam.

'He's lying in the hallway. He won't get up.' There was an unfamiliar note of concern in Mickey's voice. Krippendorf climbed out of the bath, wiped his eyes, and wrapped a towel around his steaming torso. A trail of imperfect footprints registered his hurried passage along the hall and down the stairs.

Edmund was lying face down near the front door. His eyes were closed and one arm was crooked awkwardly beneath his thin chest. There was an unnatural flush to his cheeks and his breath came in quick rasping snatches. Krippendorf knelt beside him and placed a palm against his hot forehead. He turned as Mickey approached clutching something behind his back. 'What did you do to him?'

'Nothing, honestly.'

'Were you playing political prisoners?'

'Not today.'

'Mickey, you must tell me.'

'I just found him lying there. I never touched him.' Mickey suddenly burst into tears. The last time Krippendorf had seen him cry was over a year before when Shelley had donated his shrapnel collection to Oxfam.

'This is not a good time to cry. Where is Mrs Guntrip?'

'She's giving Shelley her enema,' Mickey sniffed. 'Can't you hear?'

Krippendorf gently lifted Edmund up and half-walked, half-ran with him to the car. He could feel the towel loosening around his waist as he went. He laid his son full length on the back seat of the car, resting his head on a bundle of unidentifiable clothing. Three times he switched on the ignition and three times it failed. He shut his eyes and gripped the steering wheel as though attempting to wrench it in two. He whispered something to the spirit of the car and tried the ignition once more. The starting-motor coughed uncertainly and he struggled to keep it alive by an effort of will. It went completely dead. After two more attempts he got the starting handle from the boot and began to crank the engine violently.

'Excuse me, Mr K.,' said Mrs O'Shea from her first-floor window.

'Not now, Mrs O'Shea.'

'It's about Mickey and that new airgun you bought him.' Her head seemed to be growing among the geraniums in the window box.

'Some other time.' He flung the starting handle aside, not intending it to land in her dried-up ornamental pond. After a moment's hesitation he lifted Edmund out of the back seat and headed for the nearby junction.

Mrs O'Shea parted the geraniums and called out, 'Have you seen what he's done to my garden gnomes?'

There were no taxis in sight. The sun shone in an almost cloudless sky, warming his back and his bare legs. Bits of gravel and soft tar were sticking to the soles of his feet, causing his toes to curl up protectively. An old man went puffing by on an ancient tricycle. Krippendorf walked into the middle of the road directly in the path of an oncoming Datsun. The car swerved sharply and mounted the pavement before coming to a noisy halt. The driver lowered the window and thrust his head and shoulders out. 'Are you fucking ga-ga?' he yelled. His fleshy pink face was twisted with shock and rage.

'I need to get to the hospital,' Krippendorf said. 'I can show you the quickest route.' Shampoo was still dripping down his face and onto his hairless chest.

The driver re-started his engine. 'Get knotted,' he said.

Krippendorf leaned into the window until his face was level with the driver's. Gripping Edmund firmly in one arm, he thrust the other inside the car. 'Feel the edge of my hand,' he said. 'It is like tempered steel. With one swift blow I can snap your windpipe.' He seized the driver's collar and tie and twisted them into a tight ball around his fist. Buttons fell away and the driver's face became a darker colour. 'All right, all right,' he choked. Still in Krippendorf's powerful grip he reached behind and unlocked the rear door. Krippendorf climbed in and cradled Edmund in his arms. 'First left, then left again,' he said. 'Please be quick.'

The driver reversed off the pavement and drove up to the traffic lights.

'Keep going,' Krippendorf ordered.

'Are you blind? It's on red.'

'Just keep going. I shall go for your jugular if I must.' He drew the edge of his hand across the roll of pink fat above the driver's collar.

The car moved forward into the path of a laundry van. The woman van-driver braked quickly and blared her horn. She leaned out of the window, put a forefinger against her temple and rotated it back and forth.

In the high street the car became immobilized amid the rush hour traffic. Krippendorf watched expressionless as the crowds jostled and pushed their way to the Underground entrance in pursuit of normal lives. A cement truck edged forward alongside the car, its huge front wheel inches from Krippendorf's face. Poisonous fumes came through the window and Edmund's breathing seemed to be getting noisier and more erratic. He looked down at the hot triangular face and realized with sudden clarity that his son was about to die in his arms. There was a smudge of chocolate or Marmite at the side of his nose and a small jagged tear in the knee of his fairly new cords.

The traffic was moving again. 'Turn left here,' Krippendorf said.

'For Christ's sake, man, it's a pedestrian precinct.'

'Do it.'

The car bumped over the decorative cobblestones of the shopping mall and the driver sounded his musical horn as he navigated slowly between concrete tubs of fuschia and elderly ladies pushing shopping bags on wheels. Some of the shops had goods displayed outside in large wire baskets and from the interior of others came the sound of harsh and unnecessary music. A man in a white apron slapped the roof of the car angrily as it passed his stall, and a woman with two children in one pram threw an ice-cream cornet at the windscreen. The driver's neck and shirt were soaked in sweat.

'Left here, then sharp right,' Krippendorf said as the painted cobbles gave way to tarmac. Edmund's breathing had almost stopped. 'Please go faster,' he said.

They found themselves in a one-way street, travelling away from the hospital. Tall billboards flanked the street on either side, all advertising the same gaseous drink.

'Stop the car and turn around.'

'Turn around? It's a fucking one-way street.'

'Please do not argue.'

The car shot forward at speed. 'I've had about enough of you,' the driver said. He crouched well forward in his seat, away from Krippendorf's hands. They passed a milk float and a three-wheeled invalid car and then the road ahead was clear for several hundred yards. Krippendorf seized the driver's hair and wrenched his head back with sudden force. The car swerved across the road and bumped the kerb before the driver regained control.

'We nearly had it then, you fucking lunatic!' the driver screamed. With his head pulled back, and his arms at full stretch, he brought the car to a standstill in the right-hand lane. Krippendorf dragged him by his hair across to the passenger seat and then clambered into his place behind the wheel. With a grating of gears he reversed the car and drove back up the one-way street with two wheels on the kerb. He kept his hand pressed on the musical horn all the way.

The rear entrance of the hospital was on the opposite corner of a busy junction. He stopped the car and once again gathered Edmund in his arms. The bath towel had fallen from him in his struggle with the driver. He walked into the slowly moving traffic, picking his way between the bumpers as though he were invulnerable. A truck driver leaned out of his cab and gave a long wolf whistle and the passengers in the lower deck of a number fourteen bus rose from their seats to get a better view of the naked figure walking on his toes.

At the rear entrance to the hospital pickets were handing out leaflets. A man with a red armband blocked Krippendorf's way as he made for the battered swing doors. The doors had strips of metal fixed along the bottom in order to be kicked.

'You can't go in there, Sunshine,' the man with the armband said. He had thick sideboards of uneven length. Krippendorf brushed past him and went through the swing doors, back first.

'You're supposed to have a chitty,' the man shouted.

He found himself in a huge deserted kitchen that for some reason reminded him of the engine room of a ship. Trays of cutlery were laid out along a wide zinc counter and saucepans were hanging on the wall in descending order of size, as though for some vaguely musical purpose. The huge empty vats had no obvious connection with food or its preparation.

Corridors led off the kitchen in several directions. Each corridor was painted a different colour, conveying valuable information to those who knew the key. He followed the lilac corridor. Enormous pipes coated with dust hung from the low ceiling and the windows were too grimy to see through. Edmund was getting heavy in his arms. He came to a ward at the end of the corridor and pushed the door open with his foot. There seemed to be flowers everywhere. He walked up and down in search of an empty bed. They were all occupied by very old women with blankets pulled up to their chins. Most of them appeared to be asleep but one or two followed him with their eyes as he went by. He laid Edmund down at the foot of a bed whose occupant took up only the top half. There was no sign of a doctor or a nurse. It suddenly occurred to him that they might be on strike.

'Hello?' he called out. 'Is anyone here?'

The air was heavy with the smell of antiseptic and decay. 'Hello, hello, hello,' he shouted. The old woman in the bed next to Edmund bared her gums in what might have been a smile. He raised his voice once more but there was no sound or movement other than the crackle of sheets and a dry whimpering cough. He picked up an enamel bedpan and began hitting it against the radiator pipes. Heads turned slowly on their oversize pillows, like the heads of tortoises.

A door opened at the far end of the ward and a nurse appeared carrying a clipboard under one arm. She came towards him quickly with a bobbing movement, the soles of her shoes squeaking on the rubberized floor.

'Just what do you think you're doing?' she hissed. 'Who are you? Get back to the men's ward at once.' She averted her eyes from his nakedness.

'My son is ill, please call a doctor.' He pointed to the bed where Edmund lay motionless on his back.

'How dare you come crashing in here like a hooligan. Can't you see this is a geriatric ward?' Her fierce whisper sounded much louder than a normal voice.

'Just call the doctor, quickly.'

'Leave this ward immediately.' She pointed to the door with her clipboard. 'You'll have to go to emergency, the same as everyone else.'

Krippendorf clenched and unclenched his hands. He went to the nearest bedside table and picked up a vase of evil-smelling flowers. For reasons unclear to himself he first tipped the flowers out before flinging the vase at the window. The glass exploded. He went to the next bedside table, raised another vase, and smashed it to the floor. Someone near the door was screaming in a thin voice. Krippendorf went along the row of beds smashing vases one by one. Blood was soon running from his feet. It left a dark meandering trail on the highly polished floor.

He was surprised to find two male nurses holding on to him. They stood one on either side of him, each gripping

141

him by an arm, firmly but gently, as though teaching him the steps of a Greek dance. 'All right, my old son,' one of them said cheerfully, 'let's all go and have a nice cup of tea.'

A doctor in a fawn turban was bending over Edmund. He was holding Edmund's wrist and pressing a stethoscope against his pale, delicate ribcage. The doctor said something to the nurse with the clipboard and she drew a screen around the bed. Krippendorf allowed himself to be led away to a dingy room at the end of the corridor and supplied with tea and machine-sliced bread. There was no taste in his mouth. He was unsure how and why he came to be wearing undersize pyjamas and a hairy dressing-gown. Someone had bandaged his feet and encased them in carpet slippers. He was aware mainly of the curtain fluttering at a barred window and the thunderous ticking of a quartz clock. Presently he rested his head on the table and went to sleep.

He was awakened by a hand on his shoulder. The doctor in the fawn turban was standing over him. He looked tired and grave. He kept his hand on Krippendorf's shoulder in a gesture of commiseration. The sound of the quartz clock filled the small room.

'Your lad is OK now,' the doctor said. 'You can see him if you like.'

Krippendorf stared at the bandages on his feet. 'You mean he is alive?'

The doctor laughed medically. 'He's got a bad dose of food poisoning. We'll need to keep him in for a few days.'

'I am forever telling him not to scavenge in the school dustbins.'

They walked side by side through corridors of various hue on their way to Intensive Care. The doctor walked slowly because of Krippendorf's feet, although Krippendorf felt no pain.

'We shall be sending you a bill,' the doctor said in his grave way. 'It could be a tidy sum.'

142

'Is he having private treatment? I have no ideological objection, of course.'

'For the damage you caused.'

'Ah.'

'You may not receive it for some time because of the postal strike.'

They stood to one side to allow a stretcher to be wheeled past. Krippendorf caught a brief glimpse of a grey face and shaven head above the red blanket. At the entrance to Intensive Care the doctor took his leave. 'Goodbye,' he said. Krippendorf tried to think of something adequate to say. He watched the doctor walk jauntily away down the long emerald corridor until he turned the corner.

Edmund was sitting up in bed, engrossed in a comic. He held it close to his eyes and moved his face from side to side as he read. His father had to address him several times before getting a response.

'They made me sick on purpose,' he complained. 'They put a rubber tube down my throat and pumped water in.'

'You would be well advised not to reveal the technique to Mickey.'

A teenage boy in the next bed had a plaster cast around his neck and chest. He was holding a mirror in front of him and decorating the plaster with coloured swastikas. Further along the ward a man with tubes in his body was shuffling up and down holding a plastic container that was slowly filling with his own yellow juices. Visitors were sitting at several of the beds. They fidgeted with their hands and looked at the clock as they tried to think of things to say to people they had known all their lives.

Krippendorf noticed the Thai nurse the moment she entered the ward. He watched with growing interest as she went from bed to bed recording temperatures. She had a tiny nose and almond eyes with an epicanthic fold. When she came to Edmund's bed, Krippendorf gave her his best smile and tightened the belt of his hairy dressing-gown. 'I am pleased my son is in such good hands.'

She ruffled Edmund's hair playfully. 'He's a good little boy,' she said. Her own jet black hair shone beneath the wings of her starched cap. Krippendorf noted with satisfaction the straightness of her back and the contours of her mouth. Yes, he thought.

'Goodbye, Edmund,' he said later to the back page of the *Beano*. 'I intend to visit you every day. Try not to get better too soon.'

The moon shone that night like a new silver coin. In the pale metallic glow the terraced houses looked strangely two-dimensional, like the backdrop for a modern ballet. Although the weather was still humid even the highest bedroom windows remained securely shut. There were almost no lights to be seen and it was eerily quiet except for a dog barking in the far distance.

Krippendorf opened the back door and crept into the garden with as much stealth as he could manage on bandaged feet. At the side of the failed marrow bed he arranged a dozen or so housebricks to make a low plinth which he covered with a damask cloth. On this he placed a large baking tray containing a crumpled up copy of the *Radio Times* and a partially defrosted chicken. At the side of the baking tray he put a carving knife. He surveyed the darkened windows all around him as he made the final adjustments to his flowing black kimono and scarlet tennis headband.

It was customary among the Shelmikedmu to make a sacrificial offering to the Moonspirit in gratitude for its benevolent intervention in human affairs. In olden times the offering was either a captured enemy or an elderly widow whose protective witchcraft substance had evaporated, but nowadays certain ritual substitutes were permitted.

144

Krippendorf sprinkled a handful of sea-salt over the chicken and then set light to the pages of *Radio Times* on which it was resting. When the flames of the pyre were at their peak he closed his eyes, spread his arms, and cried out in a tremulous voice, 'Oh wondrous and omnipotent Moonspirit be praised! Blessed are Thee for extending Thy protective hand to the child Edmund in his hour of mortal danger. Let the soul of this creature now before me fly to Thee on the wings of our obeisance. *Na kuqr mxplottx unq shelxmuk klk hrnqlum.*' He picked up the carving knife and plunged it into the chicken's breast. The knife quivered as it struck first the bone and then the giblets still frozen in their polythene bag. He then drank a libation of Algerian red wine from a pewter goblet and uttered a final prayer. When the ceremony was over he washed the chicken under the tap and put it in the refrigerator for Sunday's lunch.

Veronica telephoned while he was working on the problem of Shelmikedmu incest preferences.

'I'll have to be brief,' she said, 'there's a crowd of drunken reporters waiting to use the phone.'

'Where are you, Kuala Lumpur?'

'Port au Prince.'

'Of course.'

'Look, I'm going to be in this God-forsaken place longer than I thought. Things are really coming to the boil. The guerillas have just captured the main barracks.'

'Hng.'

'It's virtually a state of siege.'

'So it is here,' Krippendorf muttered. 'On a purely domestic level.'

'What? I can barely hear you.'

There was a noise on the line as of Manchester United

football supporters roaring through a tunnel in pursuit of Manchester City supporters.

Presently he heard Veronica say, 'Jamie, did you hear me? How's the housekeeper making out? Is she getting things under control?'

Krippendorf drew back his upper lip. 'Mrs Guntrip is having a marked effect upon the children.'

'Thank God for that. I was afraid she might find them too much of a handful.'

'They are beginning to speak with a Rhondda accent. They now refer to luncheon as dinner and call napkins serviettes. I fear they may soon become completely proletarianized.'

Veronica clacked her tongue. 'Now don't start all that,' she warned. 'I'd like a quick word with her. Please put her on.'

Krippendorf shook his head. 'I fear that is impossible. It is Thursday here.'

'Jamie, it's Thursday *here*. It's Thursday every-bloody-where. So what?'

'On Thursday evenings she attends her seance. She is in regular weekly communion with Mr Guntrip, who seven years ago fell off a slag heap near Blaenau Ffestiniog.'

There was a brief silence on the line, followed by a series of muffled thuds.

'Can I hear mortar fire in the background?' Krippendorf asked out of mild interest.

'No, it's these bloody reporters banging on the door,' said Veronica, just before the line went dead.

The sun continued to shine from an almost cloudless sky. Articles appeared in women's magazines advising secretaries how to avoid sweating in the office and a Minister of the Crown appeared on peak-hour television requesting people not to panic and to turn off dripping taps.

Because of the heat, Krippendorf kept the fanlight

window in his study permanently open, though his door remained firmly shut. He was now recording the complexities of Shelmikedmu syntax for the sake of posterity. He stuffed a wad of cotton wool inside his upper lip, pressed the record button of his cassette, and commenced reading backwards from the current issue of the *Beano*.

Soon it grew dark. He attended to his work with total concentration, pausing only occasionally to mop the perspiration on his forehead with a pad of blotting paper. While he was illustrating the uses of the future subjunctive there was a loud explosion somewhere below and immediately the lights went out. He spent several minutes feeling for his matches and a candle.

'Jim-Jam,' Shelley called. 'You'd better come down. Something's happened.'

He peered into the darkness. 'Where are you?'

'With Mrs Guntrip.'

He found Shelley and Mickey whispering excitedly in the doorway of the housekeeper's room. Mickey was flashing the beam of his commando torch across the ceiling and down the walls.

'What are you doing?' Krippendorf said. 'Where is Mrs Guntrip?'

'Just there, look.' Mickey shone his beam on the rotund shape lying diagonally beneath the bed.

'Whatever happened?' Krippendorf bent forward, advancing his candle. There was a smell of must.

'It was Mickey,' Shelley said. 'He did it while Mrs Guntrip was saying her prayers.'

'Did what, for goodness sake?'

'He plugged her hearing aid into the mains.'

Krippendorf encircled Mrs Guntrip's plump wrist with his thumb and middle finger. 'Is that true, Mickey?'

Mickey's voice assumed its familiar defensive whine. 'I was only practising. We're doing circuits at school with Mr Warburton.'

Krippendorf said sternly, 'It was an extremely thoughtless act. Now you see the full consequences. You have blown all the fuses. How on earth do you expect to get your science O-level?'

Shelley reached forward in the dark and touched her father on the elbow. 'Jim-Jam, why are you talking in that funny voice?'

Krippendorf removed the wad of cotton wool from inside his upper lip, rolled it into a ball, and dropped it into Mrs Guntrip's chamber pot.

Edmund appeared, wearing only his Spiderman pyjama jacket. 'What's going on?' He shielded his eyes from the beam that Mickey was now flashing directly into them.

'Mickey's blown up Mrs Guntrip,' Shelley said, jerking her chin at the upturned feet neatly placed together.

'Is she dead?'

'Very,' Krippendorf said. The bones in his knees cracked as he straightened up.

'Should we give her the kiss of life?' Edmund asked.

'Such extreme measures are not really called for.'

They all sat on Mrs Guntrip's bed discussing the manner of her passing and its possible short-term and long-term effects.

'Is Mickey old enough to be hung?' Edmund enquired optimistically.

'Hanged,' said his father.

Mickey was making grotesque shadows on the ceiling with his stubby fingers. 'It was only an accident,' he reminded them. 'It's not my fault if her crappy old hearing aid went wrong. She should've had a Japanese one.'

'We're not telling anyone, are we?' Shelley suddenly cried out in alarm. 'I don't want people nosing about my room.'

Krippendorf tut-tutted loudly in the dark. 'This is not a matter for the authorities. It is a purely domestic affair. We have suffered quite enough external interference of late.'

The church clock struck ten. Twelve minutes later it struck the half-hour.

'What are we going to do with her?' Shelley enquired as she dangled her bare feet inches above the faintly luminous yellow pom-poms. 'In this weather she'll soon start ponging.'

'I know,' said Mickey brightly. 'We could bury her in the garden. She'd be company for Ms Molly.'

'No,' Krippendorf said decisively, 'I do not want the runner beans disturbed. It should be a good crop this year. Reading Proust to them is having its effect.'

Edmund proposed a different solution. 'We could keep her in the freezer. She won't go bad there.'

Krippendorf gave his younger son an appreciative pat on the shoulder. 'Well done, Edmund. That is the most constructive suggestion yet. It will certainly do as a temporary measure.'

After a lengthy wrangle it was finally agreed that Edmund should lead the way with the torch while the rest of them carried Mrs Guntrip downstairs. On the first-floor landing they had to stop to rest their arms.

'Couldn't we just roll her down?' Mickey panted. 'She's just the right shape.'

Krippendorf readjusted his grip on the podgy shoulders. 'Do stop complaining,' he said. 'It is not often I get you to do small chores.'

By slow degrees they struggled their way downstairs and into the kitchen. Edmund held open the lid of the freezer chest while they laid Mrs Guntrip gently across the economy packs of processed peas and tubs of raspberry ripple.

Krippendorf mended the fuses while Shelley warmed a saucepan of milk and set out the best Coronation mugs. At Edmund's prompting, she also grilled a large number of waffles and spread them with the new chocolate-flavoured crunchy peanut butter. They sat around the table, father and children, sipping Ovaltine and munching contentedly.

Presently, Mickey said, 'Can we watch the late-night

movie? It's yonks since we've been allowed to stay up after eight.' He glanced meaningfully at the freezer.

'Go on, Jim-Jam,' Shelley pleaded. 'Being as it's a special occasion.'

Krippendorf smiled tolerantly into his warm milk drink. 'Very well then. Provided it is not too violent.'

Early the following morning he was awakened by the telephone. He lay back with his eyes still closed, waiting for it to be answered. Then he remembered.

'Sorry to ring you at this unearthly hour, old boy,' Dunkerley said. 'I've been trying to get you for days. Whoever it is who answers the phone says she's never heard of you.'

Krippendorf stared at his bare white toes. 'You should have no further difficulty on that score.'

Dunkerley began enthusing about the recent batch of photographs Krippendorf had sent him. 'I'll be using at least two of them for our feature on Primitive Poppets.'

'And what about the text?' Krippendorf enquired tetchily. 'The illustrations are only intelligible when set in their proper cultural context. I have sometimes felt that your editorial cuts and revisions have been such as to rob the pictorial evidence of its scientific validity.'

Dunkerley sounded genuinely surprised. 'Have you, old boy? I'm awfully sorry. It's always seemed to me that your pictures more or less spoke for themselves.'

Krippendorf tightened his grip on the receiver. 'I also think that your tendency to re-title my articles with pithy substitutes of your own can often be misleading. For example, I do not honestly think that the gist of my analysis of uxoricide was accurately conveyed by your title, "Bumper Boobs and Bums".'

Dunkerley's voice took on an apologetic tone. 'I take your

point, old boy, but the sad fact is that most of our readers aren't mad keen on hermeneutics. They think Lévi-Strauss is a pair of jeans.'

Krippendorf passed the receiver from his right hand to his left. 'The whole point of my contributing to your journal is to bring instruction to the unenlightened. I wish to convey to others the grandeur and enchantment of anthropological discovery. If I cannot use your publication to this pedagogic end I must seriously consider bringing our present arrangement to a close.'

A heavy puffing sound came from the other end of the line. 'Now don't let's get too hasty, old boy. I'm sure we can work something out. As you know, we're very flexible here at *Exotica*. We like to accommodate different approaches, encourage different schools of thought. Only last week I commissioned a piece by a well-known Peruvian Maoist on sexual disorders among the Inca.'

Dunkerley offered some other examples of his editorial eclecticism and went on to outline his scheme for an advertising drive on breakfast television. 'I'm actually ringing about a couple of quite different matters,' he said.

Krippendorf waited.

'The secretary or someone from the Crouch End Folklore Society has been on to me. They'd like you to give a talk at one of their Thursday meetings. Apparently, some of their members have been very impressed by your stuff in *Exotica*. They'd like to know more about your tribe.'

Krippendorf smiled modestly. 'I should be only too pleased to lecture to them.' He scribbled down the secretary's telephone number on the one corner of the memory board not covered by the children's drawings of fanged and bespectacled three-legged babies.

'By the way,' Dunkerley added, 'They'd like you to show slides.'

Without hesitation Krippendorf said, 'That can be arranged.' He was already anticipating the pleasure of lecturing once again. What should he take as his central theme? Love and endogamy? Coconut symbolism in Shelmikedmu drinking songs?

Dunkerley interrupted his thoughts. 'The other thing I wanted to talk to you about is rather more urgent.'

'Mm?'

'I think I told you that we're starting up our own travel agency. The idea is to organize exclusive tours to places of anthropological interest, mainly for our readers.'

'Yes,' Krippendorf said warily.

'Well, the thing is, there's a tremendous amount of interest in your neck of the woods. It seems that lots of people are ready to part with large sums of money to go and see the . . . er . . . thingummy for themselves.'

'Oh.'

'I was hoping I could persuade you to act as a courier for a party of twelve on a three-week trip in September. You could show them round the place, introduce them to the people they've already come to know from your photographs. It could be a very cultural experience.'

Krippendorf ran his hand across the top of his head. 'I am afraid that would be very difficult.'

'Why?'

'The Shelmikedmu are not easily accessible.'

Dunkerley gave an audible groan. 'Please say you'll try. As far as expenses are concerned you can write your own cheque.'

'September is the beginning of the rainy season.'

'So? They can take umbrellas with them. They're not going there for a suntan.'

Krippendorf thought again. 'In September I go to the annual conference of Anthropologists Anonymous. It is highly therapeutic.'

Dunkerley's voice cracked. 'Couldn't you give it a miss, just this once? Don't let me down, old boy, I'm really

152

desperate. You see, the simple fact of the matter is I've already confirmed the bookings and spent the deposits.'

Mickey and Edmund were throwing bread pellets at each other across the breakfast table.

'Dad, you'd better look at the freezer,' Edmund said, casting a bread pellet in that direction. 'The lid won't shut properly. Our ice lollies are starting to thaw.'

Krippendorf raised the lid of the cabinet and gazed upon the now solid bulk of Mrs Guntrip protruding well above the recommended storage level.

'She's expanded,' Mickey explained. 'Liquid objects expand in volume when they're frozen. We did it with Mr Warburton.'

Krippendorf put on his rubber gloves and tried to rearrange the contents of the freezer so that everything would fit. Finally he gave up in exasperation. 'There is no room for Mrs Guntrip and the porkburgers,' he said. 'One of them will have to go.'

Mickey slouched across to the freezer and drummed his fingers contemplatively on Mrs Guntrip's frozen parts.

'It's her shape that's the trouble,' he declared. 'She'd fit in easily if she was in separate pieces instead of one big awkward lump.'

Krippendorf stroked his chin reflectively. 'You mean if she were to be redistributed in individual . . . joints?'

Mickey nodded. 'It would be easy with the Black and Decker.'

'Hm,' Krippendorf said. 'I suppose it is worth a try.'

They cleared away the breakfast things, covered the table with clean newspaper, and laid Mrs Guntrip on it.

Krippendorf plugged in the Black and Decker and switched on the power. 'I am not too familiar with the principles of jointing carcasses,' he confessed. 'I believe the

English method differs in important respects from the Continental.

'Mrs Guntrip is Welsh,' Edmund reminded him.

Krippendorf hesitated for a moment. 'That is a complicating factor, I agree. Nevertheless, for present purposes she could be treated as English. That is the least we can do.'

He made a few swift strokes with the hedge-trimmer, but the results were not to his complete satisfaction.

'Edmund,' he said, switching off the power. 'Fetch the old tea-towel that occasionally serves employment as Shelley's neckerchief. It is decorated with a helpful illustration of a carcass with named and numbered joints.'

'But that's a drawing of a pig.'

'Edmund, this is no time for pedantry.'

Following the diagram on the tea-cloth as accurately as he could, Krippendorf commenced the division of Mrs Guntrip into separate portions of varying quality and dimension.

'Can I have a go?' Mickey pleaded. 'It was my idea.'

Krippendorf looked at him askance. 'I am surprised you should even ask. Your recent handling of electrical equipment leaves a lot to be desired.' He moved round to the other side of the table. 'Edmund, will you please stop fooling about with that spare rib. Show a little respect.'

They wrapped the portions in plastic bags and stacked them neatly in the freezer.

'See, I was right,' Mickey boasted as the lid was shut. 'She fits in easily like that,' He sat on the lid and kicked his heels.

They heard the nine o'clock pips on Mrs O'Shea's radio. 'Oh dear,' Krippendorf said. 'You are late for school. I suppose I had better give you an explanatory note for the teacher.'

Nine

Malinowski Research Institute
Cambridge

Dear Dr Krippendorf,

The Scholarship and Scrutiny Committee have now considered your Final Report on Research Project Mal 8051/Kr entitled 'The Hegemony of Myth: Social and Symbolic Reproduction among the Shelmikedmu of the Amazon Basin'.

It is my agreeable duty to inform you that the Committee were unanimous in adjudging your work to be of the highest standard of scholarship and scientific achievement. The Committee further decided by seven votes to two (one abstention) to award you the Lévi-Strauss Memorial Prize for the most original contribution to the discipline in the past twelve months. Book tokens to the value of £17 will be despatched to you in due course.

As you are no doubt aware, the recipient of the Prize is automatically invited to address the Annual Meeting of the British Society of Structural Anthropologists. The meeting this year is to be held in the Assembly Rooms of the Colwyn Bay Co-operative Society. This Institute will, of course, be pleased to defray your travelling expenses (Second Class rail) and to arrange accommodation for you in the dormitory of the Working Men's Hostel.

In conclusion, allow me to add my own personal congratulations. I believe your remarkable study of the Shelmikedmu to be the most innovative contribution to anthropology since my own under-rated analysis of Hottentot nightmares.

I look forward to meeting you in Colwyn Bay.

> Yours sincerely,
> J. H. R. Wayneflete-Smith,
> Director and Emeritus Professor.

The hot weather continued unabated, causing widespread speculation about the behaviour of polar ice-caps and volcanic eruptions in distant lands. Policemen patrolled the streets wearing short-sleeved shirts open at the neck, watching for infringements of the water regulations. Café tables with striped umbrellas were rumoured to have appeared on the pavements in Sutton Coldfield and Bury St Edmunds, and imports of Japanese fizzy drinks broke all previous records.

Shelley said, 'We'll have a barbecue this evening. I'll do kofta à la Grecque.'

'She means meatballs on skewers,' Mickey said deflatingly, before volunteering to light the charcoal with his napalm gun.

Edmund laid the table beneath the shade of the elm tree. On his own initiative he used the plates and cutlery from the picnic basket. Soon the warm evening air was filled with the fumes of paraffin and smoking fat.

Mrs O'Shea's face appeared above the fence. 'Is the house on fire again, Mr K.?' she enquired.

'Not yet, Mrs O'Shea, merely our supper.'

'I very nearly called the brigade.'

'That was a most neighbourly thought.'

156

She disappeared from view. 'I should keep a bucket handy,' they heard her call. 'I always do when your Mickey's around.'

With their meatballs, they had a tossed green salad and long loaves of crusty bread smothered with garlic butter. A light breeze blew fitfully, rustling the leaves of the elm and sending the paper napkins floating into the neighbours' gardens. A pair of cicadas had made their home in the hawthorn bush and were sawing frantically. As they ate, Mickey told them about the failed hovercraft trip with Four B to Boulogne and the unexpected arrest of the geography mistress.

His narrative was interrupted by Edmund. 'Ergh, what's this?' he cried, spitting something into the salad bowl.

Krippendorf retrieved it and wiped it with his napkin. 'How very odd,' he said. 'It looks like part of an ear-plug.' He held it up against the pale blue sky. 'To be more exact, part of a hearing aid.'

The sounds of eating ceased abruptly. Mickey and Edmund exchanged glances.

'Shelley,' Krippendorf said, reaching for a glass of water and drinking all of it, 'I want you to think very carefully. What exactly did you use for the kofta à la Grecque?'

'A pinch of paprika, some oregano, a clove and a half of . . .'

'What meat, Shelley?'

Shelley gave him one of her looks. 'The meat in the freezer. Why, were you saving it for Christmas?'

Krippendorf stared at the two remaining meatballs on his skewer. 'Oh dear, oh dear, oh dear,' he said. He took a clean napkin and wiped his lips comprehensively.

'I didn't get it from the Co-op, if that's what you're thinking,' Shelley said petulantly.

Krippendorf placed a placatory hand on his daughter's arm. 'I am certain you did not. The origin of the kofta à la Grecque is not in contention.'

Everyone listened in respectful silence as he explained to his daughter the nature of her culinary error. It was also broadly agreed that no particular blame attached to her and that, moreover, she ought to have been fully apprised of the contents of the freezer. 'It is one of those silly mistakes that can happen in any family,' Krippendorf pointed out, 'through lack of proper communication.'

Edmund was the first to take up his knife and fork. Tentatively at first, and then with increasing gusto, he resumed his interrupted meal. 'Anyway,' he spluttered, 'I think it's scrumptious.'

Mickey quickly agreed. 'It tastes a bit like that meat you stuffed the turkey with at Easter.' He held up a meatball between his fingers and inspected it carefully, as though seeking signs of recognition.

'No, it's much nicer,' Shelley insisted. 'It's got a definite flavour of its own.'

'Children,' Krippendorf said, rapping the table sharply with his fork. 'Will you please stop referring to the housekeeper as "it". Where are your manners?'

To Shelley's manifest relief, everyone had a second helping of Mrs Guntrip, followed by tinned pineapple chunks in heavy syrup with butterscotch foam topping.

On the first day of the school holidays the children stripped the floorboards from what was once again the guest room and built a tree-house high up in the elm. They slept there at nights on beds made up from cushions taken from the settee and easy chairs. They spent a large part of the day there, too, scrambling up and down the rope ladder or hoisting up their various possessions to add individual touches of homeliness.

Edmund now began to go around completely naked

except for the leather waist-thong that his father occasionally used in his photographic work. Mickey made himself a loincloth and Shelley wore an ankle-length sarong fashioned from her straw sunbathing mat. Mickey had jeered at her the first day she appeared in it. 'Look at her two mosquito bites. Amanda Copplestone's are bigger than that, and she's only in Four B.'

As the long, hot summer days went by their colouring changed from white to pink to honey to brown. They rarely left the tree-house or the garden. A fire was kept continuously burning in the barbecue pit where Shelley did the cooking.

Krippendorf showed them how to decorate themselves with body paints in the Shelmikedmu fashion. They spent many happy hours sitting together in the sun marking their faces and bodies with Tipp-Ex and green nail varnish. When it grew dark they sat around the glowing embers listening to their father reveal the secrets of Shelmikedmu wisdom. He instructed them in the ancient rites and sacred customs as well as in the practical domestic arts. They sat in silent fascination, absorbing knowledge painlessly.

After the children had retired to their tree-house for the night, Krippendorf often continued squatting by the fire, gazing up at the stars and puffing on his long clay pipe. Late one night, as he sat alone, he heard them whispering above him.

'Not like that, Mickey,' Shelley said. 'Do it properly or not at all.'

'Shut up, I'm trying my best. It's harder for the boy than the girl.'

'You're such an awkward twit. Where's your maggot?'

Mickey let out an agonized scream.

'Don't yank it like that,' he squealed. 'It's not a lavatory chain.'

It was silent for a moment and then Shelley said, 'No, clumsy. Get your other knee right across.'

'That's not how Amanda Copplestone does it,' Mickey said.

Shelley sighed irritably. 'We're supposed to be doing it the Shelmikedmu way. Like Jim-Jam showed us.'

There followed a sound as of a bath or kitchen sink being unblocked with a rubber plunger.

'Not so loud, Mickey,' Shelley complained. 'You'll wake Edmund. And try and keep your cheesy feet out of my face.'

Krippendorf crept soundlessly away, a tall figure outlined against the night in his flowing white kimono. He felt a quiet satisfaction that the children seemed to be getting along so well together of late.

Edmund pushed away his plate of clay-baked chicken. 'Why are we having this muck?' he said grumpily.

'You like clay-baked chicken,' Shelley reminded him.

'Not any more. Why can't we have our favourite?' He twirled his finger in the bleached curly locks that now hung down to his shoulders.

'For goodness sake be reasonable,' Krippendorf said. 'We cannot have it every day. Already this week you have had Guntrip fritters, Guntrip dopiaza, and Guntrip *en croute*. You need a properly balanced diet.'

Edmund thrust his lower lip forward into a pout. 'It's the only kind of food I can eat.'

'Me too,' Mickey said. 'I get a kind of craving for it, like people do for heroin.' He fiddled with the drawstring of his leatherette loincloth.

'That's your tough luck,' Shelley said unsympathetically as she poured quantities of olive oil and wine vinegar over a bowl of sliced, home-grown tomatoes. 'We ate the last of it yesterday. You can go and look in the freezer if you don't believe me.' She sucked the tips of her fingers and wiped them on her sarong.

160

Edmund's lower lip began to quiver and then his eyes slowly filled with tears. 'I want some more,' he snivelled.

'You can't have more,' Shelley said. 'Eat your chicken. It's the one we sacrificed last night.'

Edmund folded his arms. 'I'll starve myself to death again,' he threatened.

Mickey leaned across the table and spoke softly in his brother's ear. Edmund gradually stopped crying. He blew his nose on the tablecloth and followed Mickey up the rope ladder. Krippendorf watched him as his small brown buttocks disappeared into the dense foliage. The two boys stayed in the tree-house all afternoon, hacking at something with their knives and whispering.

Veronica rang from Port au Prince while he was fitting Shelley's wooden lip-plug.

'They've just bombed the runway,' she announced. 'We're going to be stuck in this poxhole for bloody ages.'

'Hng.'

She spoke briefly about the storming of the presidential palace and the problems caused by the shortage of alcohol in the big hotels.

'I haven't got long,' she said. 'Please put the housekeeper on.'

Krippendorf looked directly into the mouthpiece. 'I am afraid that is impossible.'

'Why? It's not Thursday, so she's not at her bloody seance.'

'Both those statements are correct.'

'Well where is she? I'm paying her to look after the children.'

Krippendorf pinched the bridge of his aquiline nose. 'She is all gone. That is to say, she is no longer with us.'

'You mean she's left?'

'In a manner of speaking.'

Veronica made a puffing sound. 'When did she leave, for Christ's sake?'

'One could not really put an exact date on it.'

'Why ever not?'

Krippendorf allowed his finger to trace the honeysuckle pattern on the William Morris wallpaper. 'She left . . . in stages, as it were.'

'Jamie, what the hell are you on about?'

'It is not an easy matter to explain over the telephone. You would need to have a fuller appreciation of the wider context.'

Veronica groaned in despair. 'I give up. You can tell me the whole story when I get back. And Jamie?'

'Mm?'

'I warn you. I intend to hear the housekeeper's side of it.'

'Can I hear drunken reporters banging on your door?' Krippendorf enquired.

'No, it's mortar fire,' Veronica said, just before the line went dead.

He glanced up at his image on the security screen as he wheeled his trolley past the catfood shelves in the supermarket. He stopped at the plastic tub containing special offers and took several tins of half-priced pilchards to add to the many others already piled high in the larder. After some deliberation he also threw into the trolley a dented tin of Bulgarian plum jam in case of sudden emergencies. A few minutes later he went back and collected a battered packet of Garibaldi biscuits and a second dented tin of Bulgarian plum jam. So far he had bought none of the items on the carefully drawn-up shopping list that he had left on the kitchen table.

At the cereal shelves he faced the recurring problem of

trying to recall which of the indistinguishable breakfast foods his children currently favoured or anathematized. He inspected the backs of all the packets to compare the nature and quality of the gifts and prizes they variously offered. He chose one that offered a set of mixing bowls and another that promised a ski-ing holiday for two in the Cairngorms.

Further along, he collected several small tubs of flavoured yoghurt and one large tub of plain. At the frozen food counter he took two large bags of oven chips, a plastic sack of chipolatas, an economy-size pack of fish fingers, a solid oblong slab of strawberry mousse, and a leg of imported lamb that looked and felt like an offensive weapon used by early man.

At the delicatessen counter he was tempted by the introductory offer on Portuguese Stilton. The woman behind the counter was wearing a straw boater and a spotted bow tie. 'Anything else, sir?' she enquired. 'Vine leaves? Taramasalata? Pine kernels?'

He studied the counter. 'Do you have guava curd?'

'No, sir, we're right out.'

'Manioc whip?'

'I'm afraid not, sir. Try the Co-op.'

'Certainly not.'

He wheeled his loaded trolley down a narrow aisle stacked high on either side with alcoholic drinks. A woman with a child seated precariously in a trolley was filling the rest of it with six-pack tins of claret and litre bottles of Korean whisky. He was agreeably surprised to find that bin ends of Ockfener Bockstein Spätlese 1976 were selling at ten per cent off. He took two bottles and then went back for the remaining two. This reminded him that Ribena figured prominently on his forgotten shopping list, as did crunchy peanut butter and banana fudge topping.

He made a final tour of the shelves in the hope of spotting other things they badly needed. He then agonized over

which of the several long queues to join at the checkout.
Fifteen minutes later he was transferring tins of pilchards
and Bulgarian plum jam from his trolley to the moving belt.
When the transfer was almost complete, the girl behind the
till said, 'This is the express checkout. Only eight items or
under.' She pointed to a sign above her head and folded her
arms.

Krippendorf re-loaded his trolley and trundled it to the
back of another queue. Twenty minutes later the checkout
girl handed him a very long slip of paper and said,
'Twenty-seven pounds, thirty-six pee.'

He wrote in the amount on a cheque which he had already
signed and dated.

'Cash only at this checkout,' the girl said. She pointed to
a sign above her head and folded her arms. Krippendorf put
away his cheque book and took out his wallet. It contained
nineteen pounds. He made a quick calculation and returned
the four bottles of Ockfener Bockstein Spatlese and the
Portuguese Stilton, unaware of the tutting and grumbling of
the people in the queue. When he was loading the shopping
into the car he suddenly remembered they needed sugar,
milk and bread.

On returning home he was surprised to find the freezer
already full. A pair of white bunny rabbits, their bodies still
slightly warm, had been laid across an indeterminate
number of colourful budgerigars.

'Shelley,' he called, and went quickly into the garden.
She was squatting cross-legged by the hawthorn bush
stringing together a necklace of teeth and small bones.

'Shelley,' he said, allowing his annoyance to show, 'can
you kindly tell me what the neighbours' domestic pets are
doing in the freezer?'

She looked up at him as though he were being deliberately obtuse. 'What d'you think? Where are we supposed to keep provisions this weather? If you think I'm
going to salt them or smoke-cure them . . .'

164

'Shelley, my question relates to the matter of *how* rather than *why* they have come to be where they are.'

She narrowed her eyes as she threaded a fine cord through a hole drilled in a tooth. 'The boys put them there,' she said.

'When?'

'After they'd come back from their hunting expedition.'

'Hunting?' Krippendorf exclaimed. 'If Mickey has been using his airgun after I expressly forbade . . .'

'Calm down, Jim-Jam,' Shelley said, sucking the thread into a point. 'They didn't take the airgun. They used their new blowpipes. The ones they made from their school recorders.'

Not completely mollified, Krippendorf swished his foot back and forth in the long dry grass. 'They should not have gone hunting,' he said sulkily. 'They know very well that is a strictly female activity. Besides, what are we going to do now with all these beef chipolatas?'

Ten

The Crouch End Folklore Society held its Thursday evening meetings in a nearby polytechnic. Krippendorf arrived early for his lecture and passed the time wandering about the bustling forecourt examining the notices and posters that covered every available inch of wallspace. On Friday lunchtime, Kevin Boxe was introducing a public forum on 'Insurgency in the Home Counties: The Way Ahead'. Clashing with his own lecture this evening was another entitled 'Homemade Pasta'. The poster advertising this had been put up in such a way as to obscure the notice of his own talk, which now read:

> ppendorf
> orial
> uctural
> ikedmu of Ama-
> 27th
> p.m.
> strated
> lcome

The forecourt became noticeably busier as people hurried purposefully to the lifts and stairs, so that after a while he felt himself to be the one constant element in a continuous sea of flux. Presently a man in a seaman's jersey approached him and said, 'Excuse me, are you Mr Tubney?' He looked at a slip of paper in his hand. 'For the lecture on Merleau-Ponty and the Welsh Question?'

Krippendorf drew back his broad shoulders. 'My name is not Tubney. I am here for a quite different purpose.'

The man seemed at first disinclined to accept this disavowal but then went off muttering and tugging at his seaman's jersey.

Krippendorf stood idly by as, one by one, people came up to the broken coffee dispenser, inserted coins in the slot, pressed the appropriate button, waited, pressed the button again and again, struck the machine with a flat hand, cursed silently, and walked away in defeat. The response to the machine's failure, he observed, invariably followed the same sequence of emotions: expectation, anxiety, disbelief, frustration, anger, and resignation. Were there the makings of a scientific monograph here?

'You must be Dr Krippendale,' said a voice at his side. 'I'm Dorothy Pike, vice-president of the Crouch End Folklore Society.' She thrust forward a stumpy hand.

Krippendorf bowed imperceptibly, like a tennis champpon in the presence of minor royalty.

'I hope I haven't kept you waiting.' She had a firm handshake, consistent with her symmetrical jaw and policeman's haircut. 'Our president, Lady Fortran, sends her apologies. She's otherwise engaged, on government business.'

'I quite understand.'

'She's opening a new soup kitchen in Leighton Buzzard.'

They worked their way through the crowd to the one functioning lift. At the foot of the stairs a man dressed in fashionably baggy shorts was selling copies of the *Gay Monetarist*. Miss Pike talked freely, in a loud voice, as though they were alone. She articulated each word with precision and much expenditure of muscular effort. 'It's such a pity we have to hold our meetings in this dreadful place. We used to use the Baptist Hall before it became a refuge for battered wives.' People in the lift stared at her more in curiosity than disapproval. Many of them were clutching textbooks to their bosoms in the manner of American high school students portrayed in black-and-white films. The lift refused to go beyond the second floor and they walked the rest of the way up.

The small windowless lecture room was almost full and Krippendorf felt a slight tremor of apprehension as he surveyed the rows of attentive faces. They looked mostly middle-aged, but there was a group of young people in the front row with notebooks open on their laps. His eyes fell upon a heavily-bearded man who was sitting by himself at the back. He had the menacing appearance of an eminent scholar waiting his opportunity to denounce heterodoxy or dilettantism.

Miss Pike banged her gavel before making her introductory remarks. 'It is with the utmost pleasure that I welcome our speaker this evening, Dr James Chippendorf, one of our foremost young experts on Amazonian savages. Dr Chippendorf has spent many years documenting the social customs of a most unusual tribe called the . . .' She held a scribbled note at arm's length from her face and squinted at it. 'Called the . . . er . . . Shell Mex, is it? At any rate, I gather that they are a most fascinating people whose way of life is of great importance to contemporary folklore science. We may ourselves have something to learn from them. I like to think that the ways of people even in far-off Amazonia, however barbaric they might seem, could possibly have some small lessons for the way we conduct our lives here in Crouch End.

'Dr Chippendorf is at present completing his *magnum opus* on the subject and we all look forward with great anticipation to its publication. Meanwhile we are privileged this evening in being offered a foretaste of what is to come. The title of his talk is, I believe . . .' Again she tried to decipher the scribble. '. . . Aspects of . . . um . . . Morris

Dancing . . . or is it Motor Racing? . . . among Snow-donians. The speaker will be illustrating his talk with the aid of the projector. Miss Doberman, perhaps you would kindly extinguish the lights.'

There was a desultory patter of applause as Krippendorf rose to his feet and switched on the small lamp above the lectern. He felt reassured by the surrounding darkness and the quite authority of his own voice as he set out his general thesis concerning the presentation and consumption of food as a form of socio-drama.

'Shelmikedmu principles of alimentary classification follow, in modified form, the standard binary pattern. The mutually exclusive categories they use are not the raw and the cooked, or the sweet and the sour, or the fried and the mashed, but *nhuqrm* and *nhaqrm*. Unfortunately, there is no exact English translation of these two terms. Very roughly speaking, foodstuffs that fall under the heading of *nhuqrm* are those of smooth and creamy texture, such as mango fool and manioc whip. Foods classified as *nhaqrm*, on the other hand, are those of lumpy and fibrous texture, such as cayman loaf or hummingbird rissole.'

As Krippendorf warmed to his theme his voice took on a note of urgency as though he feared there might be insufficient time for him to get the full force of his message across. He glanced at his watch. It surprised him to discover that he had been talking for twenty minutes without yet having reached the structuralist core of the argument. The audience were beginning to show signs of restlessness.

'I'm not sitting here all bloody night listening to this,' someone mumbled.

'Be quiet, Malcolm.'

'We've missed the bloody football now.'

'Shush.'

'I said we should have gone to the one on volcanoes.'

Someone near the front was snoring softly and someone

else was rustling a bag of boiled sweets. Krippendorf paused for a moment to wipe his brow and to pour scummy water from the bakelite carafe into a crumpled paper cup. At his side, Miss Pike was busily making notes on the back of a printed leaflet calling for an immediate investigation into the library deaths.

He cleared his throat and continued. 'One somewhat unusual feature of Shelmikedmu commensal practices is that the classification of foods is bound up with the rules of social exchange. That is to say, all dishes classed as *nhuqrm* must be passed around in a clockwise direction, and all the dishes classed as *nhaqrm* must be passed around anti-clockwise. If any foodstuff is inadvertently handed round the wrong way it at once becomes contaminated and must be buried in the ground. My houseboy on one occasion ate from a bowl of witchetty-grub dip that had been passed to him anti-clockwise by mistake. When he discovered the error he was violently sick upon the spot.'

'When's he going to show the bloody pictures?'

'Do be quiet, Malcolm.'

Miss Pike leaned across and slipped a message on the lectern. It was written in capital letters and said, 'I can allow you another fifteen minutes. The room is booked for nine o'clock by the karate club.'

He took another sip of lukewarm water and put aside the next ten pages of his lecture dealing with the military consequences of food poisoning. 'By way of conclusion,' he said, 'I should like to offer one or two brief observations on Shelmikedmu cuisine. The first point to be borne in mind is that although men do the actual cooking, women play a leading part in preparing the raw materials for the kitchen. It thus falls to a man's wives or daughters to strip the puma skins, pluck the macaw feathers and finely chop the coconut.' He switched on the projector and inserted the first slide. 'Here you can see a young woman pounding cassava roots for her father.' A collective gasp rose from the men in the audience as the frontal view of the Ethiopian babysitter flashed up on the screen.

'Jesus, what a pair!'

'Oof, oof.'

'Sit down, Malcolm.'

'And here you can see the village headman's senior wife whipping goat's milk.' Again there was a sharp implosion of breath as the screen lit up with a picture of the Thai nurse kneeling on a strip of rough matting and holding something shadowy in her hands. Someone started clapping and the students in the front row were stamping their feet. But the loudest acclamation of all was reserved for one of his early studies of Melba mixing the guava curd.

'*Mama mia*,' someone cried. A chair went over with a crash as people from the back surged forward for an unobstructed view.

'Order, order!' Miss Pike called out, banging her gavel repeatedly. 'Will you please sit down at once and clear the aisles. You are in breach of the fire regulations.'

Krippendorf prepared his next slide as Miss Pike's voice rose above the hubbub. 'Miss Doberman, be so good as to switch on the lights. Someone is liable to get injured.'

It was several minutes before everyone was re-seated and the noise had died down. 'We have only seven minutes remaining,' Miss Pike said reproachfully. 'If the speaker is willing I propose that we devote them to our customary question time.' She glanced sideways at Krippendorf who nodded his assent. He sat down, shuffling his notes like a television newscaster.

'Now,' Miss Pike enunciated, 'who would like to put the first question?' A dozen hands shot up. 'Mr Cripps, I think,' Miss Pike said, pointing her gavel at a man with a cigarette behind his ear.

'What I couldn't make out,' Mr Cripps said, 'was why

171

these people chucked grub away just because some twerp passed it the wrong way round. I mean to say, there couldn't really be anything wrong with it, could there?'

Krippendorf stifled a sigh. 'I thought I had made it quite clear. Any infraction of the rules governing the circulation of food necessarily results in its contamination.'

Mr Cripps shook his head vigorously. 'I don't think you follow my point, Squire. What I'm saying is that it couldn't *really* go bad just because of that. It stands to reason.' He turned to face the audience as though to enlist support for his case.

Krippendorf closed his eyes and did not open them for four or five seconds. 'The food becomes ritually polluted, and therefore inedible.'

'But it can't do,' Mr Cripps insisted..

'Yes it *can*,' Krippendorf snapped.

'It bloody well can't, it's impossible.' shouted Mr Cripps, causing spit to fly from his mouth onto the hat of the lady in front.

Krippendorf jumped to his feet and gripped the sides of the lectern so that it rose fractionally off the table. 'It can and it does,' he said between his teeth. 'That is what Shelmikedmu believe, and that is what counts.'

'Well they must be sodding thick,' retorted Mr Cripps.

Miss Pike banged her gavel. 'Thank you for your contribution, Mr Cripps. You may sit down. Next question please.' She surveyed the raised arms and flapping hands. 'Yes, Mr Lopta.'

'Could we please see the slides again?' Mr Lopta said. 'There was one in particular . . .'

'Certainly not,' Miss Pike said. She looked at the wristwatch propped up in front of her on its expandable metal strap. 'If there are no more questions, I should like to thank our speaker for a most . . .'

'I have a question,' said a voice from the back of the room. 'Or at least an observation.'

172

Miss Pike hesitated. 'Very well, Ursula. But please make it brief.' She tapped her wrist.

The woman called Ursula took off her spectacles and let them hang from her neck on a chain. In a worryingly deep voice she said, 'It seems to me there are a number of serious inconsistencies in your analysis, of both an epistemological and nomothetic kind.'

'Christ, she's off again.'

'Be quiet, Malcolm.'

'We can hardly take seriously an account of Shelmikedmu commensalism that completely ignores the work of Ungoed-Jones. His interpretation of the rituals you have described is infinitely more persuasive than your own. You have dealt simply with surface phenomena. Ungoed-Jones goes beneath appearances to the underlying essence, to the very nature of things.'

Krippendorf stared at her in astonishment. 'I had no idea Ungoed-Jones was an authority on the Shelmikedmu.' He took out a handkerchief and wiped his palms.

'He most certainly is.'

'Do you happen to know when he did his fieldwork?' We might have met.'

She gave a brief, dismissive laugh. 'Fieldwork is unimportant to his method. He has unmasked the universal laws dictating all forms of commensality from the Shelmikedmu wedding feast to the English Sunday breakfast. The structure of any meal can be shown to conform to the same triadic formula. Allow me to illustrate.' She walked briskly forward to the blackboard, picked up a handful of chalks, and drew two white circles inside a green triangle.

At that moment the door was flung open and half a dozen men dressed in karate kit came bounding in. They stopped suddenly in their tracks, embarrassed by the rows of staring faces. 'It's nine o'clock,' one of them said sheepishly.

'By my watch there is still a minute and a half to go.' Miss Pike thrust out her symmetrical jaw. 'However, this seems an opportune moment at which to bring our meeting to a close.' She stood up and waited until the room was completely quiet before saying, 'On behalf of all members and guests of the Crouch End Folklore Society I should like to thank Dr Chippendale for a most informative and stimulating talk. I know that I speak for all of you when I say that the things we have heard and seen this evening will remain in our memories for a long time to come.' When the applause had died down she said, 'Let me just remind you that next week we have Mr Osberton, who will be addressing us on the Problem of Polynesian Basketry.'

Miss Pike led Krippendorf back down the teeming corridors to the entrance of the hall. People were pushing past them in all directions. Within the space of three minutes they were invited to buy copies of the *Home Counties Insurgent*, *Pottery World*, and *Seventh International*, as well as being asked to sign a petition calling for the lifting of the curfew in the Crouch End area.

'As a matter of interest,' Krippendorf said, 'who was the woman who spoke so knowledgeably about Ungoed-Jones?'

Miss Pike gave an uncontrolled laugh. 'You mustn't mind Ursula,' she said, laying a hand lightly on his arm. 'She makes the same speech every week.'

'And who exactly is Ungoed-Jones?' he asked. 'I am not familiar with his work.'

'Nor is anyone else. Only Ursula seems to have heard of him. It's all she ever talks about.' Miss Pike looked furtively over her shoulder and then said in her closest approximation to a hushed voice, 'Frankly, between you and me, I think he's nothing but a figment of her imagination.'

'Pass the milk,' Mickey said, elbowing his brother. Edmund pushed the bottle towards him with the blade of his knife.

174

'No,' Krippendorf said loudly. 'That is the wrong way. How many times must I explain? All things that are poured are passed from right to left. All things that are shaken are passed from left to right. Milk, water and Ribena go one way. Salt, pepper and tomato ketchup go the other. It is all perfectly simple.'

Edmund pushed the milk bottle towards his father who then moved it on to Mickey. 'There, now it will not turn rancid.'

Mickey poured himself a glass of milk and said, 'I'm never sure about the tomato ketchup. When it's full we pour it, but when it's nearly empty we shake it.'

'Precisely,' his father said. 'That underlines my point. The thing being passed is not itself the determining factor. What matters is not the substance *per se*, but whether at any given juncture that substance requires to be poured or shaken. No contradiction whatsoever is entailed in circulating the tomato ketchup in different directions according to changes in its viscosity and hence in its logical status.'

Eleven

September began with a flurry of light showers that did no more than dampen the surface of the baked, cracked earth. Then the warm weather returned, causing renewed speculation about the effect on the atmosphere of nuclear tests and aerosol sprays.

Veronica returned home on the day of the ice-lolly murders. She rang from Heathrow while Krippendorf was mending the totem pole. 'I know it's a terrible drag, Jamie, but I'm taking straight off again. I'm going to Tehran to cover the women's riots.' The pips went prematurely and he waited for her to feed in more coins. 'My flight's at six this evening. That'll give me just enough time to pop home to see the kids and clean myself up. We might even get in a quick poke.'

She arrived an hour later in a taxi bearing a garish advertisement for a recently collapsed building society. Krippendorf carried her bags in and poured her a long drink. 'Christ,' she said, sprawling in a chair and tipping back her head. 'It's hotter here than in Port au Prince.'

Krippendorf said, 'The outlook is for continuing high humidity with the possibility of thunderstorms later in the west, spreading east by morning and clearing later in the day.'

Veronica fanned her face with a yellowing copy of *Psychic News*. 'Are you cool in that rig-out?' she asked, eyeing him obliquely. 'The taxi driver wondered if you were rehearsing for *Aida*.'

Krippendorf's eyebrows formed a pair of arcs below his scarlet tennis headband. 'Really? Allusions to high culture are not the usual ingredients of lower-class repartee.'

Veronica chatted for a while about the many difficulties encountered in trying to film the execution squads and about the behaviour of journalists deprived of drink.

'How are the kids?' she said, holding out her glass for a refill. 'I've really missed them.'

'They are in very good form. It has been quite an eventful summer for them, one way and another.'

'Did you go anywhere? Kos? Herne Bay?'

Krippendorf locked his hands together and placed them behind his head. 'They could not be persuaded to take a conventional holiday. They seemed perfectly content to make their own amusement here.'

Veronica inclined her head in surprise. 'That's an encouraging sign. It sounds as though you've managed to get things together at last.'

She levered herself out of the armchair and unzipped one of the many zips on her khaki valise. 'I've got some presents for them. Are they around?'

Krippendorf said, 'You will most likely find them in their tree.'

'What?'

'The elm tree. They live there more or less permanently now.'

Veronica paused for a moment at the door, as though expecting further elaboration, before making her way to the garden. Moments later Krippendorf heard the rise and fall of her voice. He rinsed her glass and emptied her ashtray.

'Jamie,' she called shrilly. 'What the *hell's* going on here?'

He dried the glass and replaced the clean ashtray on the coffee table.

'Jamie,' she called again. 'Will you please shift your butt and come out here.'

He found her steadying the rope ladder while Edmund

climbed slowly down. 'Jamie,' she hissed, 'what's been happening here while I've been away?'

'Happening?' Krippendorf allowed his gaze to wander round the garden at the shrivelled runner beans and cankered hawthorn.

'Look at the *children*, man. They look like bloody savages.'

She grabbed Edmund firmly by his arms as he jumped off the rope ladder. 'What's this in your hair?' she demanded. 'And this shit all over your body? You smell like a Turkish sewer.'

Edmund struggled to get free. 'It's not shit,' he protested. 'These are my clan markings. I'm in the junior Anaconda clan.'

'Clan markings?' Veronia said through clenched teeth. 'I'll give you clan markings across your bum.' She frogmarched him to the back door and pushed him in. 'Get straight to the bathroom and scrub yourself clean. When you've washed that sheepshit out of your hair go round to the barber's and get it cut. He'll probably have to use a rotary mower.' She slammed the door and stalked back to the elm tree.

'Come on you two,' she shouted up. 'Get yourselves down here. Let me have a proper look at you.'

Mickey's face appeared over the edge of the platform. 'Hello, Mum,' he grinned.

Veronica gasped and pressed both hands against her face. 'Mickey, what's happened to your teeth?'

Mickey drew back his lips to afford a fuller display of his finely pointed incisors. 'I've filed them,' he said. 'I used your manicure set.'

'Jesus Christ.' Veronica turned angrily. 'James, did you let him do this?'

Krippendorf was removing wrinkled brown leaves from the stem of the dying clematis. 'It is a common practice in many parts of Amazonia,' he informed his wife. 'Its purpose is mainly aesthetic, but it does have certain practical advantages. Among some tribes . . .'

'We don't live in fucking Amazonia,' Veronica screamed. 'We live in fucking Islington. Though I'm beginning to doubt it.' She tugged violently on the rope ladder as though hoping to bring the tree-house crashing down.

'Come on, Shelley,' she cried. 'It's no use hiding up there. Either you come down or I'll come and fetch you.' She placed one high heel unsteadily on the bottom rung of the ladder.

'I'm not hiding,' Shelley replied calmly from behind a partition of sacking and torn blankets. 'I'm busy. I'll be down later.'

Veronica said on a note of sarcasm, 'What are you doing, making a feather bloody head-dress?'

'Don't be silly,' Shelley replied haughtily. 'You're confusing us with Plains Indians.'

Veronica tried a more conciliatory approach. 'Darling, please come down. I haven't seen you all summer. Tell me what you've been doing.'

'I'll be down shortly. I've nearly finished.'

'Finished *what*, for Christ's sake?'

Shelley said, 'I'm weaving a *hloxroq* for my *kinkru*.'

Veronica's face looked as it generally looked when she examined the engine of the car. 'I can't make head or tail of what you're saying. Are you stoned?'

Shelley said slowly and with great precision, 'I'm weaving a back-sling for the baby.'

'Whose baby?'

'Mine, of course.'

'Shelley, you *are* stoned. You haven't got a bloody baby.'

'I shall have in April. I've decided to have it underwater.'

Veronica let go of the rope ladder and took one step backwards. Her mouth opened and closed like the mouth of a swimmer in a heavy sea. It was several seconds before she could say, 'Jamie, is this her idea of a joke? She's not really up the spout, is she?'

Krippendorf stepped over the neatly tended grave of Ms Molly and scattered slug pellets around the last surviving clump of French marigolds. Without looking up from his task, he said, 'All the signs appear to be positive: the cessation of the menstrual cycle, a palpable augmentation of witchcraft substance, an insatiable craving for humming-bird dip. . .' He gathered up a handful of dead snails and tossed them under the hawthorn bush.

Veronica said, almost to herself, 'Jesus, I can't believe all this.' She walked unsteadily into the house, holding one hand a little in front of her as though feeling the way in the dark. Half an hour later she came out wearing a different dress but the same grim expression on her face. 'My minicab's here,' she said with demonstrable self-control. 'I'll be gone for about a week. That gives you plenty of time to get this lot sorted out. When I get back . . . Jamie, are you listening?'

Krippendorf was twisting small pieces of green wire around the stems of Mrs O'Shea's climbing yellow roses, training them to grow along his own side of the fence.

'Mm?'

'I said when I get back I expect to see the children looking like human beings again. I want them out of the trees, scrubbed, de-loused and dressed in clothes. All this *Lord of the Flies* stuff is finished. Understood?' She cast a final glance over her shoulder. 'Christ, and I thought Haiti was primitive.'

He waited until her minicab was out of sight before ringing Dunkerley.

'Hello, old boy. Funny thing, I was just about to call you.'

'Oh? If it concerns my article on foot fetishism . . .'

'No, no,' Dunkerley interjected, 'nothing to do with that,

the pictures were fine. Actually, what I wanted from you was a decent map of central Amazonia and detailed instructions how to find this blasted tribe of yours. There's no mention of them in the *Oxford Ethnographic Atlas*.'

'Hng.'

'The first tour is due to leave next week. Frankly,' he groaned, 'I'm dreading it. It'll be like the Burma campaign all over again.'

'You intend to lead the . . . expedition yourself?' Krippendorf said in some surprise.

'I'll bloody well have to,' Dunkerley wailed. 'No one else would take it on.' There was a momentary silence before he said weakly, 'I don't suppose you'd change your mind? I'd be prepared to double the fee.'

Krippendorf cleared his throat. 'As a matter of fact my circumstances have changed somewhat since we last discussed the matter.'

'You mean . . . ?' said Dunkerley with bated breath.

'I am now in a position to accept the assignment. That was the purpose of my call.'

Dunkerley gurgled with joy. 'That's marvellous, that's absolutely fantastic. I can't thank you enough, old boy. I tell you what, you can have the entire December issue of *Exotica* to yourself. Fill it with any structuralist rubbish you like.'

When Dunkerley had calmed down a little, Krippendorf said evenly, 'There is one small point I ought to mention. I shall be accompanied by my three children.'

Without a second's hesitation Dunkerley said, 'No problem. No problem at all, we've got bags of spare capacity. Take the wife too if you want. Give her a break from the kitchen.' He babbled on at length about visas and typhoid injections and how to evade the new currency restrictions. Before ringing off he said, 'I hope your kiddies will like it over there. Do you think they'll adjust all right to the primitive life?'

Twelve

Stormclouds were gathering in the sky above Heathrow as the battered green minivan screeched to a halt at the entrance to terminal three. Dunkerley jumped nimbly from the driver's seat, hurried to the rear of the van and opened the doors with a flourish. 'Chop, chop, gentlemen, let's be having you,' he yodelled. 'Adventure awaits, ha, ha.'

Inside, the six men half-sitting on the rough wooden benches let out a whinnying cheer and stamped their feet on the rolling floor of empty Heineken cans. The stocky man sitting furthest from the doors adjusted his sombrero and tucked his Hawaiian shirt inside his grey flannel trousers. 'Hey up, young Trevor,' he bellowed jovially, 'shift your fat self. And while you're about it button up your flies. You're not in the bloody jungle yet.'

The man called Trevor gave an undulating, bronchial cry and beat his fists against his chest on either side of the Pentax camera dangling from his neck on a tartan strap. He doubled up in a fit of coughing before he could say 'Me, Tarzan.'

One by one the six men clambered out of the van puffing and swearing amiably as they dragged out their heavy suitcases and army surplus tents and loaded them precariously on the one available trolley. Tied to each piece of luggage was a cardboard tag bearing the inscription *Exotica Tours: Shelmikedmu Expedition No.1*.

Dunkerley fussed about ticking off names on his computer print-out and distributing mosquito nets. He also handed each man what appeared to be a school lunch-box.

'Your survival kit. Inside you'll find malaria pills, a compass, a ball of string, an AA map, a bar of plain chocolate and a nailbrush. No, Mr Outhwaite,' he sighed, 'don't eat the chocolate now.'

They steered the loaded trolley erratically through the swirling crowds in the check-in hall, losing two members of the party on the way. Dunkerley checked the names on his computer print-out. 'Mr Bragg and Mr Palethorpe are missing,' he announced glumly.

'No, I'm Mr Palethorpe,' said Mr Palethorpe, pointing to himself. 'I'm here.'

'It's Mr Bragg and Mr Colclough what's missing,' observed the man in the sombrero. 'There's nowt to fret about, they got their compasses.'

Swearing softly but intensely to himself Dunkerley climbed on the luggage-trolley and surveyed the mass of moving bodies. Presently he spotted them. 'Over here, gentlemen,' he called, flapping his handkerchief at the two gangling men identically dressed in khaki shorts and white plimsolls who had attached themselves to a party of Korean plumbing engineers bound for Johannesburg.

'Wake up, Braggo,' jeered the man called Trevor. 'Wrong bloody tribe, you soft slummock. Them's Nips.'

Dunkerley's face grew increasingly haggard as he struggled to keep his party together and shepherd them safely through check-in. He was visibly relieved to see standing at the entrance to passport control a tall, upright man in a fawn linen suit who was holding conspicuously in front of him a back number of *Exotica*.

'Dr Krippendorf, I presume?' He extended his right hand and mopped his face with his left. 'I am so very glad to meet you.'

Krippendorf bowed his barely perceptible bow.

'Deceptive things, telephones,' Dunkerley laughed. 'I pictured you as someone with a big bushy beard and a denim suit and CND badges, ha, ha.'

Krippendorf sucked air in sharply through his flared nostrils. 'Hng,' he said. He rolled his copy of *Exotica* into a tight cylinder and dropped it in one of the futuristic litter bins.

'My apologies for being late, old boy,' Dunkerley said in a half-whisper. 'I had to keep stopping on the motorway every ten minutes to let this lot pee or be sick. I hope for your sake the second leg of the journey is easier than the first.' He unfolded his computer print-out and showed Krippendorf the list of names, two of which had been crossed through in red. 'When we started off this morning there were eight of them,' he explained. 'But one absconded with a petrol pump attendant and one fell out of the van somewhere between Doncaster and Worksop.' He looked thoughtful for a moment and then said chirpily, 'Anyway, never mind about that, let me introduce you to the surviving members of the expedition, all of whom are also on the central committee of the Pontefract Flyfishing Association.'

One by one the members of the Association stepped forward and identified themselves.

'Lionel Outhwaite,' said a man in a Fair Isle jumper. 'Grand to meet you.' He gripped Krippendorf's hand powerfully in both his own. 'I'm your number one fan, me. I've got all your photos pinned up in me locker.'

Krippendorf beamed down at the man's plastic Grecian sandals and woolly socks. 'I am delighted to hear it. I have always held that anthropology could be made intelligible to the lower orders.'

The man wearing the sombrero doffed it as he stepped forward. 'How do?' he said breezily. 'Hapgood's the name. Howard Wesley Hapgood.'

Krippendorf shook his hand warmly, observing as he did so the thick encrustations of coaldust beneath the huge fingernails. 'Your first trip to Amazonia?' he enquired.

'Him?' wheezed Mr Bragg derisively. 'Ama-bloody-zonia? It's his first time past bloody Cleethorpes.'

'Shut your gob, Braggo,' said Mr Hapgood amicably. 'I would have gone on that day trip to Llandudno, happen I hadn't been on manking picket duty.' He took a swig from his Heineken can and passed it to Mr Palethorpe who emptied it in a single gulp and then pushed both fists into his stomach to expel the gas. 'Don't suppose they sup our kind of brew where we're going,' he burped ruefully.

There was a sudden commotion at the far end of the concourse, beyond the cafeteria. Edmund came scampering along pulling excitedly at his leather g-string, his otherwise naked body gleaming with sweat.

'Bloody hellfire,' exclaimed young Trevor. 'Look on bloody Mowgli.'

Edmund pushed his way urgently through to his father. 'Mickey's shot another Arab,' he announced breathlessly. 'But only in the leg.'

Krippendorf raised his eyes to the ceiling. 'The tiresome child. What is it this time, a Shi'ite or a Sunni?'

Just then his elder son appeared through a crowd of giggling Burmese nuns. He was glancing nervously over his shoulder and trying unsuccessfully to conceal his blowpipe beneath his skimpy leatherette loincloth.

'Mickey,' said his father gravely, 'you must immediately cease all hostilities against members of the Muslim faith. We have no doctrinal quarrel with Islam.'

Mickey's irregular features arranged themselves into the familiar pattern of injured innocence. 'Anyone would think I did it on purpose,' he whined. 'I was aiming at the security guard.'

The Burmese nuns parted ranks once again, this time to reveal a burly man in black and white robes. Shouting incomprehensibly, he limped towards Mickey with surprising speed and seized him by the throat. As if responding to a pre-arranged signal, all six members of the Pontefract Flyfishing Association moved in on the man, grabbing handfuls of his robes.

'Hey up, Rudolph Valentino,' said Mr Colclough with quiet authority. 'Where d'you think you flaming are, Leeds United?'

The man at once released his grip on Mickey's throat, lifted up his robes, and pointed to a tiny puncture in his calf just above his sock-suspender. His guttural tones rose higher and higher in the universal cadences of wrath.

'It wasn't one of my poison tips,' Mickey said reassuringly from behind his father's back.

Mr Palethorpe unbuckled the straps of his Home Guard knapsack and took out a tin of band-aids for use in tropical climates. 'Keep yourself still, and stop your mithering,' he said as the Arab winced pneumatically. 'What d'you expect, a sodding pay-bed?'

Still complaining bitterly in a foreign tongue, the injured man hobbled away, not quite turning his back until he was out of Mickey's range.

Mr Hapgood was practising on the blowpipe with spent matches. 'Handy little beggar,' he said reflectively. 'Just the job for use against the police horses.'

The Burmese nuns filed past in twos on their way to the departure lounge. Each pair turned to giggle at the sight of Edmund picking absent-mindedly at the Tipp-Ex markings on his semi-erect maggot. Over the public address system what sounded like an urgent message in Tamil or Swahili was barely audible above the noise of shouted farewells in many other languages.

Dunkerley looked ostentatiously at his watch and handed Krippendorf a manilla folder decorated with the abstract logo of Exotica Tours. 'Passenger list and travel documentation,' he said airily. 'Don't get lost, and bring them all back alive, ha, ha.'

Trevor nudged Dunkerley with his Heineken can. 'You not coming with us, matey?' he asked in a tone of incredulity.

Dunkerley backed away. 'No, no, no, no, no. I'm leaving

you in the hands of the expert.' He pointed to Krippendorf with his chin. 'He's the only man in England who knows where to find these people.'

The members of the expedition gathered their things together and followed Krippendorf past the armed guard and into passport control. 'Bon voyage,' Dunkerley called after them. 'And bring me back lots of lovely pictures.'

Shelley had been in the departure lounge most of the morning. She was now squatting inside a makeshift hut constructed of upturned seats and cardboard boxes from the duty-free shop. She scraped a dark gelatinous substance from a pot and rubbed it into her hair, indifferent to the stares of the many people who peered inside and occasionally flashed their cameras.

'It's not very comfy,' Mickey complained, as he and Edmund crawled in through the narrow entrance. 'It needs more foam cushions.'

'Piss off, you two,' Shelley yelled. 'Go and build your own camp, there's plenty of stuff around.' She lashed out with her feet at the two intruders. The ramshackle structure began to rock to and fro as the primordial struggle over property rights became increasingly physical.

Krippendorf reached into his back pocket for his notebook as he observed the scene professionally. 'Their behaviour is altogether different in the elm tree,' he pointed out to Mr Bragg. 'How interesting that Heathrow should bring their aggressive instincts to the fore. It throws new light on the heredity versus environment debate.'

Mr Bragg nodded in agreement and fingered the buckle on the thick leather belt that held up his khaki shorts. 'My two was just the same. I used to give them a right good larruping every day, no matter what. It did them no end of good – they're both in cavity insulation now.'

A muffled scream came from inside the hut and almost at once Mickey came scuttling out. 'I got the bitch that time,' he grinned, licking specks of blood off his finely pointed teeth. He went running off in search of movable building materials. 'Nothing too elaborate,' Krippendorf advised. 'Heathrow is only our transitory encampment.'

He strolled over to the duty-free shop with Mr Bragg to join the rest of the contingent. Each member of the expedition was carrying a wire basket loaded with boxes of coronas and litre bottles of Glenmorangie.

'Aye, aye, Mr . . . er . . . Thingy,' called Mr Colclough. He picked up a bottle by the neck and flourished it like a tennis racquet. 'What's the duty-free allowance for Amazonia?'

Mr Hapgood snorted derisively from behind a display of British sherries. 'They don't have customs and excise in the jungle, you big pillock. Tek all you can bloody carry.'

Krippendorf felt a light touch on his elbow. He looked round and then down at the diminutive figure of Mr Palethorpe. 'I've bought these trinkets to give to the natives,' he said, grinning sheepishly. 'To use instead of money, like.' He held up a string of coloured beads, a crested shoehorn and an assortment of chromium-plated jam spoons.

'Good idea, lad,' boomed Mr Outhwaite. 'I think I'll take them chockies. They have a very sweet tooth, do savages.' He added to his basket a gift-wrapped box of liqueur chocolates and several cartons of After Eights. 'Come to think on it, they'd probably prefer Black Magic.'

Krippendorf made one or two purchases of his own and wandered across to the bookstall where he soon became engrossed in a paperback novel that claimed to have been shortlisted for an obscure prize. He was in the middle of chapter three when an announcement caught his attention. 'Final call for flight BA 667 to Rio de Janeiro. Boarding at gate twenty-two. Final call.' The message was repeated once more in English and once in Portuguese. He replaced the novel on the gardening shelf and went in search of his party.

Shelley had dismantled her camp and was now busy painting orange and blue tribal markings on Trevor's pitted face. 'It's to ward off the evil eye,' he explained solemnly. 'I'm not taking no bloody chances, me.'

Edmund was sitting on Mr Colclough's knee wearing Mr Hapgood's sombrero while Mr Palethorpe showed him a trick with his false teeth and a rubber band. Krippendorf scanned the departure lounge for actual or circumstantial evidence of Mickey's presence. A small knot of people had gathered in a far corner of the lounge near the Disabled lavatory. As he approached he could see thin wisps of smoke rising from an unidentifiable source. He found Mickey kneeling behind an empty wheelchair fanning a pile of faintly glowing embers with a cafeteria tray.

'Why on earth are you lighting a fire?' Krippendorf enquired, genuinely puzzled.

Mickey did not look up. 'To cook dinner, of course. I'm not eating that muck on the plane.'

'Not dinner,' his father said irritably, 'luncheon. I do wish you would master the difference.' He took Mickey powerfully by the arm and pulled him away from the smouldering heap of car-hire brochures and sandwich wrappings. As he did so a woman in a fluffy white track-suit tiptoed cautiously forward and poured a glass of Babycham over the embers, causing them to hiss.

Krippendorf shouldered his bag, raised his right arm high in the air and swung it forward and down like a subaltern leading his platoon into enemy fire. The members of the expedition gathered up their knapsacks and duty-free purchases and followed him in a straggling line through the departure lounge and down the long glass passageways leading to gate twenty-two.

Edmund was sitting astride Mr Hapgood's shoulders

and waving his sombrero at the armed sentries stationed every hundred yards. 'Hey up,' he called to each of them in turn.

Shelley was walking arm in arm with Trevor and teaching him to count to ten in Shelmikedmu. 'You're wasting your time, lass,' Mr Palethorpe said. 'He can't count beyond four in bloody English.'

Trevor made a gesture with his thumb and forefinger. 'Well their method's a lot easier,' he sneered. 'They've got nowt but even numbers.'

On the other side of the glass partition passengers from an incoming flight were streaming along in the opposite direction. Krippendorf glanced at his watch and urged his dawdling party on to greater efforts. As he was passing the multilingual rabies warning he heard someone banging violently on the partition. He looked round and was surprised to see Veronica. She had her face pressed against the glass and was mouthing inaudibly and jabbing her forefinger like a trade union militant haranguing the rank and file. Krippendorf stared straight ahead and quickened his pace. From the corner of his eye he could see his wife scurrying along a yard or so to his left. She was dragging her shoulder-bag by the strap and slapping the glass ineffectually with her free hand. He turned right into a completely deserted passageway festooned on either side with unsubtle advertisements for accident and life insurance.

'Did you see that mad bint?' panted Mr Bragg, almost running to keep up. 'She were trying to bite her way through the chuffing plate-glass.'

Krippendorf shrugged. 'Airports have that effect on certain types of personality. I am already collecting data on the problem.'

The party re-grouped by degrees at the security check, where Mickey incurred official displeasure for pushing Edmund through the baggage X-ray in order to see whether any of his organs was missing or deformed.

'I'll die of cancer now,' Edmund sobbed, 'before we even get there.'

The wide-bodied aircraft was only a quarter full and the members of the expedition spread themselves out comfortably along the entire back two rows of the smoking section. Shelley and Trevor sat huddled together away from the main body of the group. Shelley's eyes shone with pedagogic zeal. Trevor listened in fascination to everything she said, his freshly-painted mouth hanging ajar.

'Keep your manking hands off her grass skirt, Trevor,' counselled Mr Hapgood from the opposite end of the row. 'It'll play havoc with your asthma.'

Trevor pointed a warning finger. 'Just you be careful. One word from me and you'll get a dose of her withccraft substance. You won't know what bloody hit you.'

A stewardess appeared in the aisle and began miming the use of an oxygen mask, slightly out of time with the gabbled Portuguese recording. Presently the aircraft was taxiing slowly backwards past grubby catering vans and parked ambulances. Krippendorf stared out of the window at the desolate grey buildings and the even greyer sky. As the nose of the aircraft swing cumbersomely round, the main terminal building came slowly into view. Among the people standing on the observation roof he caught sight of a smallish, compact woman with bright auburn hair. She was standing on the bottom bar of the safety fence and pumping both arms up and down simultaneously.

'Children, wave goodbye to your mother,' he said, pulling down his window blind. 'And Mickey, stop inflating all the life-jackets. We may very well need them.'

Moments later the aircraft was roaring down the runway and then rising steeply over the pebble-dash houses and the reservoir. Mr Colclough sucked illicitey on his duty-free Havana and waved it above his head. 'Hey up, Amazonia!' he cried in jubilation. 'Here we bloody come!'

The wings tilted alarmingly as the aircraft began its wide

sweeping arc to the south-west. Soon the no-smoking signs were switched off and then the drinks-trolley was being rattled along the aisle. High above the yellowing fields of Dorset, Edmund's tremulous voice rose and fell in farewell song:

> *'Shelmikedmu ki qumlo*
> *prnk i ga*
> *Skrmu liqniq mu hoxlo*
> *o nhumux ka.'*

The members of the Pontefract Flyfishing Association set their drinks down on their seat-trays and clapped. 'I'm going to learn some songs like that, am I,' declared Mr Outhwaite as he wiped froth and peanut crumbs off his lips with his forearm. 'That's the whole bloody point of a culture trip.'

'He's quite right,' said Mr Palethorpe meditatively. 'We can do our bit too. We can teach the little buggers "Ilkley Moor".'

Rain streamed diagonally up the windows as they passed through banks of dense cloud. Despite the turbulence, Krippendorf arranged his seat in the reclining position. He unlaced his shoes, plugged in his headphones and fiddled with the channels. He declined the proferred tray and readjusted the air-vent above his head. After a while he draped his handkerchief over his face and settled down to what he felt might be a long and eventful journey.